I0728214

The Missing Link

A Novel

Revised Edition

Adam S. Pfeffer

Ocala, FL

Zeta Publishing, Inc
3850 SE 58th Ave
Ocala, FL 34480
www.zetapublishing.com

This is a work of fiction. All the characters, names, incidents, organizations, and dialogue in this novel are either the products of the author's imagination or are used fictitiously.

Ordering Information:
Quantity sales. Special discounts are available on quantity purchases by corporations, associations, and others. For details, contact the publisher at the address above.
Orders by U.S. trade bookstores and wholesalers. Please contact Zeta Publishing: Tel: (352) 694-2553; Fax: (352) 694-1791 or visit www.zetapublishing.com

First published by iUniverse in 2007

Rev. Date: 6/13/2017

ISBN: 978-1-947191-04-4 (sc)

ISBN: 978-1-947191-05-1 (e)

Library of Congress Control Number: 2017942560

Printed in the United States of America

To My Parents

The tendency to aggression is an innate, independent, instinctual disposition in man.

—SIGMUND FREUD

The loathsome cruelty of mankind to man forms one of his inescapable characteristic and differential features; it is explicable only in terms of his carnivorous and cannibalistic origin.

—RAYMOND DART

Introduction

This is a story of what could possibly be. It concerns genetic engineering, biotechnology, the human genome, and what makes a human being a human being. Scientists are trying to decipher who we are and where we came from using the genetic code. This is a story of what could possibly happen in obtaining those answers. Whether it could happen, there is no doubt. Experiments are going on all the time utilizing the theories and materials described in the following story. Whether it will happen is altogether another question.

The latest development in this search for the origins of the human being is the discovery of a key gene that helped the human brain evolve from our chimp-like ancestors. The gene, called HAR1F, may provide the answer why human brains are triple the size of chimp brains. The work was being done by a team led by study co-author David Haussler, director of the Center for Biomolecular Science and Engineering at the University of California, Santa Cruz.

In just a few million years, one area of the human genome seems to have evolved about 70 times faster than the rest of the genetic code. This apparently helped in tripling the size of the human brain's crucial cerebral cortex.

The study looked at 49 areas that have changed the most between human and chimpanzee genomes. They succeeded in finding an area with "a very dramatic change in a relatively short period of time."

The gene didn't even exist until 300 million years ago and is present only in mammals and birds, not fish or animals without backbones. There are only two differences in that one gene between a chimp and a chicken. But there are 18 differences in that one gene between human and chimp and they seemed important in the development of man.

The dramatic change in the gene in humans is attributed to the stress of getting out of trees and walking on two feet. The gene is apparently also involved with the cerebral cortex, the site of the more complex brain functions, including language and information processing.

The gene, however, is only one part of the mystery that is the human being. The following story deals with what could happen in attempting to solve that mystery. As stated in the book, the most important discovery of the nineteenth and twentieth centuries was surely DNA. It alone has helped us attempt to unlock the mystery of life on this planet. What that will lead to is another question. The following story illustrates what some of the possibilities may be. Whether it will lead to evolutionary monsters running around is anybody's guess. One hopes science will be more responsible with the knowledge and not use it to create mutated creatures. The experiments, however, are going on at this moment and many of those mentioned in the following story, are taking place right now. Whether all the things mentioned in *The Killer Ape* become fact, only the future knows.

The time to think about the future, however, is now.

NEW YORK

September 6, 2016

Chapter One
Ngila

I am a monster. Or so they say. I don't remember where I was born or when. I guess that doesn't matter. I am a man. Yes, Ngila is a man. I have the dream. I am in the jungle by the side of a gleaming silver stream. I look around, but see only the bubbling stream. It is peaceful here. Like home. And then I see the ape creature standing beside the stream. He bends down to drink and I step into the light.

"I am a man," I say to the ape.

He looks at me, growls, and then hurries off into the bushes. I begin to grunt, throw my arms into the air, and shout towards the top of the trees.

"I am a man," I shout.

I then turn around and see many apes standing by the side of the stream. They growl at me, and I shout back that I am the rightful ruler of the jungle. Then I see the apes are holding stones, and they begin to throw them at me. The stones hurt me as they hit my body. I see the apes sneering and howling at my presence. I snarl at them, but the stones keep flying through the air.

"I am a man," I shout at them.

They don't listen to me, and keep throwing the stones. Then I turn and run towards the trees, disappearing into the bushes. The apes are still howling in the distance. I keep running, until finally, the trees are no longer there. I am now standing in the middle of a paved avenue.

"I am a man!" I shout.

I turn and see two bright lights charging towards me. I look into the light, and there is the sound of a car horn. I snarl, but the lights come towards me. It is then I open my eyes and realize I am still lying on the ground in the middle of the park.

It is then the old man comes back. He is wearing a strange look on his face. He turns back towards the darkness, and begins to speak.

"There's your monster, officer, just as I said," he says.

There's a man in blue, a police officer, who steps out of the darkness holding a gun in his hand. I snarl, lunging towards the two men, and bite into the old man's neck. I knock the police officer to the ground and I run. I keep running until I hear the sound of an explosion. Something tears into my skin, and pain shoots through my body like the sting of a thousand bees. I keep running, not letting myself fall, and I jump behind some bushes.

When I reach the trees, I look at my arm, and see there is blood. There is the sound of another explosion, and a bullet hisses among the leaves and branches. I look at my arm, the blood oozing from a small hole in the sleeve of my black coat. I wait for a moment, listening for any more explosions, and then I hurry off into the darkness.

Chapter Two
Hudge Stone

I first heard about the monster while working at the *Herald*. I had recently joined the paper's night police beat, reporting on everything from robbery to murder. Although the work was interesting at first, filled with a variety of experiences that seemed to give one insight into the human condition, the constant occurrence of crime eventually made the job somewhat routine. I had learned how to suppress my emotion, become stoic enough to face the horror of death without flinching, and then calmly gather the necessary facts. The only moments I really felt any sensation seep into my brain, my bones, was when interviewing grieving relatives of a victim, or after completing a particularly interesting story. The rest was strictly by rote.

Well, anyway, I was in the midst of working on a story involving a stabbing, one in which the victim had received minor injuries, when the phone began to ring.

"Stone speaking," I said.

There was a prolonged pause, someone breathing on the other end, and then a raspy voice began to whisper. "I seen that monster roaming around the park tonight," the voice said.

I listened to the words and couldn't help frowning. "Central Park?" I asked.

"Near the lake," was the reply. "He disappeared behind some trees."

I didn't know what to think. Then I thought I'd try to trick him with the next question.

"Did you notice what he was wearing?" I asked.

"A long, black coat," came back the reply.

Then I hit him with the trap. "Then why do you think it was a monster?" I asked.

I heard the man coughing on the other end, the noise of the phone being fumbled, and then a click and the dial tone. I placed the phone down, took a deep breath, and then swiveled back in front of my computer.

This wasn't the first time I had heard about the monster. Rumors of some sort of monster had been going around for a while, with wild speculation added with each reciting. It had become something of a running joke among the New York press, an unsubstantiated rumor that lent some levity to an otherwise solemn job. But thus far, there hadn't been one body found attributed to the deeds of any monster, and according to the police, it was nothing more than an amusing hoax.

Still the rumors persisted. Some said the monster was a man who had been badly disfigured in some ghastly factory accident, others swore he had been deformed at birth and discarded by his parents, only to be raised by the homeless as revenge against the human race. None of the rumors were ever verified, and were subsequently dismissed as hearsay.

I had completed my story for the next day's paper when I decided to check the paper's files, "the morgue" as it was called in newsroom lingo, for recent crimes in Central Park. I still was not sure what I was looking for, but, at least, I would familiarize myself with the facts.

The first clipping concerned a thirty-three-year-old man who was murdered in the park while out for a walk. According to the story, it occurred sometime after seven in the evening, and the cause of death was determined as strangulation. The victim was found with bruises on his neck, chest, and arms.

The next incident occurred a few days before at about five in the evening when a twenty-eight-year-old woman, walking her dog, was robbed and raped. A few days before that, someone grabbed a six-year-old boy in the park who was later found lying among the trees and grass. I read the clippings carefully, noting the age of each victim and the time at which the crimes reportedly took place.

There was another story about a twenty-four-year-old man who was fatally stabbed after eight in the evening; a homeless woman who was raped as she slept near the park skating rink; a thirty-two-year-old piano teacher who was beaten during an attempted rape in the early evening hours, and a twenty-year-old woman who was killed while jogging in the northeast corner of the park.

I paused for a moment to unfold one clipping that included a map of the park. "Central Park is eight-hundred-forty-three acres of bucolic splendor in the midst of New York City," it read. It showed the park stretching from Fifty-ninth Street to One Hundred-and-tenth Street, including a skating rink, a zoo, an open-air theater, athletic playing fields, meadows, fountains, a lake, a reservoir, ponds, and even a castle.

The park was first conceived in the 1840s by poet-editor William Cullen Bryant and architect Andrew Jackson Downing, and in 1853, the state Legislature decided to make it become reality. In 1856, the land was finally bought for about five million dollars. A plan by the architects Frederick Law Olmsted and Calvert Vaux was then chosen from among thirty-three submitted, and they were subsequently awarded the two-thousand dollar prize. The clearing of the site began in 1857, and after millions of cartloads of dirt and topsoil, the planting of about five million trees and shrubs, and the construction of roads, bridges, and arches, the park was completed in 1873 and officially opened in 1876.

The police, of course, maintained the park was perfectly safe. The clippings proved otherwise. Through the years, it had become a haven for murderers, rapists, and now so-called monsters. As I walked back to my desk, I began to wonder whether this current transgressor was actually a composite of all the people who had recently committed crimes in the park, or whether he was a vague sketch of a new killer on the loose. I was about to sit down and think about the possibilities when a voice crackled over the police radio frequency.

"We have a report of a missing person in Central Park," said the voice. There was a pause, amid sizzling static, and then the voice continued. "A witness reports some sort of creature—"

That's all I had to hear. I turned, raced across the newsroom, swung open a door, and rushed outside.

I jumped in my car and headed to Central Park. I soon could see police cars up ahead, their lights slashing through the darkness. A small knot of bystanders had gathered nearby.

"Any word on the victim?" I asked a police officer standing in front.

"No crime has been committed," replied the officer. "We're searching the area for a missing person."

I looked at the crowd of people staring into the darkness, doing their own search for what they believed was inside the park. "Did anybody see anything?" I finally asked.

One of the people in the crowd, a young man in black wearing white sneakers, shouted out what the rest of the crowd was thinking. "It was the monster!" he said.

I looked at one of the officers and opened my narrow reporter's notebook. "How about it, officer, is there a monster on the loose?" I asked.

The officer sneered. "You've got to be kidding," he replied. "These people don't know anything about what's going on." He then turned and directed the crowd to move away from the park.

I, however, kept walking forward. A woman with lustrous dark hair and tears running down her cheeks was standing next to one of the officers. I had a feeling she was the one who had reported the missing person.

"Stone of the *Herald*," I shouted. "Can I ask this woman a few questions?"

The officer frowned. "There'll be no interviews, Stone. She's part of official police business. And can't you see she's distraught? You guys really are vultures, aren't you? Well, you can just go back from where you came. We'll let you know if anything happens."

I remained looking at the pretty woman, but knew it wasn't worth a confrontation with the officer to attempt to speak with her, so I turned and walked back toward the knot of people still standing outside the park. I had taken only a few steps when somebody shouted amid the darkness.

"We found something," said an officer, emerging into the light.

I watched as the officer vanished once again into the shadows. I then rushed in after him, spotting him hurrying among the trees. I watched as he headed for a group of officers huddled in the darkness, and then quickly hid behind one of the trees. Two beams of light were being directed toward the ground where a motionless body, its arms and legs sprawled across the grass, lay in a dark red puddle of blood.

"This is Bombeck," said one of the officers into his police radio. "We have a possible homicide." He paused for a moment. "And parts of the body are missing, including half of the man's brain."

A few minutes later, I was back among the surging crowd of people gathered near the park. Bright television lights illuminated the scene. Many of those standing behind the reporters had been lured by the curiosity generated by tragedy.

A number of reporters jostled for position behind the yellow tape that prevented people from entering the crime area. A white sheet covered the dead man's body still lying among the trees.

"Any suspects?" shouted one of the reporters.

A detective investigating the murder approached the bright lights. "We will be pursuing all leads in an effort to find the killer," he said, amidst a throng of microphones and notepads. "Let me remind you this case is still under investigation."

"What about the monster?" another reporter shouted.

"There is no monster," replied the detective, staring into the television cameras. "And I would appreciate it if all of you would refrain from creating unnecessary panic. Now let us do our jobs and catch this killer."

He stepped back and walked away, ignoring the reporters still shouting questions amid the bright lights. I watched, standing among the crowd of reporters, as a young man attempted to push his way into the glare of the lights.

"I know what done it," he shouted. "Seen him running away."

He looked at the crowd and hesitated. Then he stared into the cameras and the words spilled from his lips. "It was the monster," he said.

Those standing nearby murmured their agreement. I jotted down the man's words, and then watched as the police officers slowly dispersed the crowd. I heard a few stragglers still talking about the monster, wondering if this was still just some creation of the scared and lonely or an actual living being. Whatever he was, he was now also a murderer.

I watched as the bright television lights dimmed and the reporters hurried away, leaving the park in darkness once more. The only people who remained were a few police officers, the sobbing woman, and a dead body lying in the glare of the crescent moon. I stood staring at the scene for a few moments, recording it all in my mind, and then headed back to the paper to file my story.

The story appeared the next day on the front page of the *Herald*. Under the headline, SEARCH FOR THE MONSTER OF CENTRAL PARK, were several quotes from police officers and city officials questioning the existence of a monster, and accounts from those who claimed to be eyewitnesses who swore they had seen a creature inside the park.

Whatever the truth was, the story caused a greater response than I could have imagined. Newsstands were flooded with anxious, interested citizens seeking any details they could find concerning the mysterious monster. Circulation soared beyond all expectations. Television and radio stations also broadcast the story, spreading it to every corner of the city. The one detail everyone seemed to agree upon, whoever or whatever the murderer might be, was that he wore a long, black coat.

After a short, restless sleep, I hurried back to the park to find out what the officers and detectives had discovered with the arrival of daylight. It was a clear day, the sun beating down upon the soaring New York City landscape. The tall buildings created dappled avenues that displayed long, blue shadows which finally vanished into columns of bright light. Among these shadows, somewhere amid the gloomy recesses of the city, a murderer was on the loose.

As I approached the park, I could see the people gathered outside on the sidewalk, still attempting to catch a glimpse of the murder scene, or even the monster himself. I noticed three children dancing wildly, alternately growling at each other.

"I'm the monster!" one of them snarled, imitating the movements of a formidable beast.

The two other children screamed in reply, and playfully began running away. "It's the monster," they screamed amid a burst of laughter.

"The monster!"

They suddenly stopped and began dancing around their small, snarling friend, reveling in his terrifying presence. "Monster! Monster!" they shouted in unison, finally ending in prolonged laughter.

I watched the display and shook my head. I was amazed how quickly the monster had become a part of youthful whimsy. If only they realized that if the monster did truly exist, there was a fearsome killer roaming the streets.

I looked at the other people in the crowd and noticed they stood searching for any sign of movement in the park. There were still a few police officers guarding the pathways, preventing people from attempting to enter. I walked up to one of them and identified myself as a newspaper reporter.

"What the hell do you want?" the officer angrily replied. "I mean, look at what you guys already started? These people actually think there's a damned monster on the loose."

"You don't believe there is?" I asked.

The officer frowned. "You would think you had better things to do than scare people for no good reason. Look at them, they're expecting to see some hairy creature with long, pointed teeth jump out of the shadows. All I want to know is, how can you print such utter nonsense?"

"Just reporting what the people say they saw," I told him.

"And they call that reporting?" he snarled. "Don't worry, Stone, we'll get to the bottom of this soon enough, no thanks to you. But don't feel bad, you can always write a story saying that someone saw flying saucers over the city. Or maybe aliens poisoning the water supply."

The officer's lips curled into a hostile sneer. He then abruptly turned away and began shouting at the crowd. "Move along! There's nothing to see here."

The day passed without a single genuine sighting of a monster. Police officials, however, knowing the murderer had only been seen at night, decided they would assign additional officers to the night shift, and attempt to apprehend him after dark. Wanting to be there when they finally captured him, I resolved I would stay near the park. That way, even if the television stations reported the story first, I would, at least, provide an eyewitness account in the next day's *Herald*.

As the day melted into twilight, with luminous orange streaks of light staining the sky, the people milling about slowly began abandoning the park and it quickly became unusually quiet. With the coming of darkness, and the monster's possible appearance becoming more likely, most of the curious bystanders apparently had decided it was prudent to seek entertainment elsewhere and in far safer quarters. It was one thing to satisfy one's curiosity, but quite another to become one of the monster's next victims. The only people who eventually remained were police officers and reporters.

Still needing a story for the next day's paper, I approached one of the officers I recognized from the night before. The officer, standing outside the park, was slightly overweight and wore a perpetual scowl as if he had surely seen too much and now suspected the entire population of criminal activity.

"What do you want, Stone?" sneered Officer Bombeck, gritting his teeth. "Don't you know there are monsters roaming around these streets, or haven't you read your paper?"

"Those eyewitnesses said they saw that monster," I argued.

"Some eyewitnesses," snorted Bombeck. "I don't take what they say very seriously especially with what our scientists found."

Now I know a good story when I hear one, so I carefully pressed for the details.

"Well, it seems the victim apparently scratched the perp, leaving a sample of blood behind," he finally explained. "And, according to our forensic people, the perp is a male human being. What do you say to that?"

"All those people couldn't have been hallucinating," I said. "Something's unique about this killer."

"Yeah, the long, black coat," he replied. "And, hopefully, he's wearing it tonight." Bombeck paused for a moment, peering into the growing darkness. "We've got to find him one of these nights," he said. "Unless he's smarter than we think and moved somewhere else to get away from all the publicity."

As I listened to his remarks, the conversation was suddenly interrupted by the sound of shouting. Bombeck turned toward his partner, and the two men began dashing down the street. I followed them until they came to a man standing in the middle of the avenue, frantically waving his arms.

"What's going on here?" asked Bombeck.

The man hurried toward them, panting excitedly. "There's a body lying in that alleyway," he said, pointing to an opening between two apartment buildings. "There's blood everywhere and the body seems to have been chopped up or something."

Bombeck raised his eyebrows and followed the man across the street. They turned into a dark alleyway, and walked another few feet.

"There it is," said the man nervously, pointing to a dark form sprawled across the pavement.

Bombeck guided the beam of his flashlight toward the mangled body. It looked almost exactly like the body I had seen the night before, except this time, the head had been completely severed from the torso. The splintered skull lay a few feet away, its contents having been confiscated.

"Call for backup," he said, turning to his partner. "That lunatic has struck again."

I stared down at the tattered body, noticing the blood, and the coarse edges on the crudely torn skin. My first thought was the body had surely been ripped apart by an extremely powerful animal.

"What kind of man is capable of doing this?" Bombeck gravely wondered.

That evening, reports of another murder were broadcast on the local television newscasts. Questions as to whether the monster had struck again reverberated across the city. Police were still baffled as to the true identity of the murderer, although they repeatedly maintained he was simply a human being and would be caught eventually. Privately, the authorities expressed outrage that he had the gall to strike again so soon after the first news reports, and at the height of citizen concern. It was as if he were mocking the concerted efforts of the police to track him down. More officers than ever had been assigned to patrol around the Central Park area, and still the murderer succeeded in evading all observation. Their only hope was that he had staked out the area as his personal territory, and like an animal, would be foolhardy enough to attempt another attack. Sooner or later, he was bound to make a mistake, and then they would have him, dead or alive.

Returning to the newspaper, I filed another grisly story. While murder of any kind was usually considered front-page material by most news editors, this one was especially significant since it marked the return of the murderer to the area. There was still much speculation as to whether he was a man, as police forensic scientists contended, or the fearsome monster as described by previous eyewitnesses. Rumors of the latter had captured the city's attention, and whether scoffed at or not, the story was the object of intense interest and debate. My editors didn't fail to take notice of the excitement and decided to assign me full time to the story until the murderer was captured. I willingly accepted, more than happy to focus my attention on the one continuing story. It was, in fact, just the break I was waiting for, and I knew if the story dragged on long enough and continued to generate reader interest, it very well could lead to a promotion, or even an editorship. That, of course, would lead to more money and a chance to finally think about settling down.

I sat and thought about the story, trying to decide on possible angles I might pursue. A police source had given me the name and address of Sandra Barton, the woman whose boyfriend had been murdered in the park, and now I planned on talking to her. I knew she had seen something that night, and although I had been prevented from interviewing her, I had a sneaking suspicion it had something to do with the alleged existence of the monster. If I was right, it would be the exclusive story I was looking for.

Grabbing my notebook and my tape recorder, I hurried off to the woman's Manhattan apartment, hoping to find her arriving home from work. The sun glowed overhead, the misty rays tumbling through banks of drifting clouds. I walked down Columbus Avenue, halted in front of Sandra's building, and then slowly stepped inside. Pressing the hallway intercom button, I waited for her to answer. After a few moments, I pressed the button again until finally realizing she had probably not yet returned from work. I decided I would wait for her outside the building, hoping to intercept her as soon as she appeared on the street. Time passed, and eventually, I crossed the street and sat down on a front staircase opposite the building allowing me to observe a larger portion of the area. I was now satisfied I would be able to spot her from whichever direction she decided to take. I glanced at my watch and realized an hour had already sped by without any sign of Sandra Barton.

With darkness soon descending upon the city, I began to get anxious that I wouldn't have a story for the next day's paper. I began to wonder whether the police would have any additional information about the murders and whether that would be enough to satisfy my editors.

I sat watching the apartment building entrance, but it was still quiet, not one person could be seen approaching. I decided I couldn't afford to wait much longer, and began preparing questions to ask the police on my return to the paper. My inquiry would concern whether any suspects had been arrested and what the coroner had concluded after examining the most recent victim.

The thought of the information I could possibly gain began to ease my mind. I would wait another few minutes, and if Sandra Barton didn't return, I would call her and attempt to set up an interview for the following day.

I looked at my watch again and noticed another hour had passed. It was getting dark now, and I stood up, preparing for the walk back to the park. I was just about to leave when I suddenly saw a woman with long brunette hair approaching the apartment building. I squinted into the dim light, and recognized her as Sandra Barton.

"Miss Barton!" I shouted from across the street, waving my arms in the air.

The woman stopped for a moment to gaze in my direction. She apparently realized she had seen me before, and raised her hand to acknowledge my greeting.

I began to hurry into the street, content that my hours of waiting had paid off. As I stepped off the curb, however, I stumbled and dropped my notebook. I turned around quickly to retrieve it, and then looked back toward Sandra Barton. She was gone!

I surveyed the front of the building and noticed a large black shadow disappearing into the nearby alleyway. I stood there staring at the building, wondering if the black shadow had snatched Sandra and taken her away. I still couldn't be sure. I didn't hear her scream for help while my back was turned, but there was no doubt that she had vanished. I thought about all the possibilities, and began to wonder whether the black shadow was actually the monster himself.

My heart began beating fast as the adrenaline began racing through my body. I tried to convince myself that it wasn't possible for the shadow to be the monster. Then I heard a faint scream in the distance. I stood frozen, looking up and down the avenue for any sign of a police officer, and then ran across the street and toward the alleyway.

I realized I was the only one who had seen the black shadow, and knew it was foolish to attempt a rescue alone. I needed some sort of assistance and, as I peered into the fading darkness, began to shout toward the windows of the nearby apartment building. After a few moments, I realized the people inside had decided to disregard my urgent plea. I knew if I left to seek help elsewhere, the monster might escape. If I didn't find help soon, however, Sandra's life may be in jeopardy. I thought for a moment, turned, and began to run back to the street. I stood beneath the streetlights, out of breath, searching for anyone who might assist me.

"Someone help me!" I shouted. "There's a woman in danger!"

I watched as the few pedestrians ambling down the sidewalk either quickened their pace away from me, or turned their heads in apparent apathy. Panting breathlessly, I stared at them with an exasperated frown.

"Don't you understand?" I said to them. "There's a woman in danger. Somebody call the police!"

Those on the street reacted as if I were requesting money. It was as if they were suddenly informed that I suffered from some rare disease. They nervously avoided me, twisting their bodies to alternate courses, while others disdainfully crossed the street.

I glanced up at the apartment building's darkened roof and listened for Sandra's voice. There was only silence, no cry of panic or appeal for help. I decided I would have to find help soon, so I began running down the street toward the park, hoping I would find police officers there still waiting for the monster's expected reappearance.

Reaching the street in front of Central Park, I spotted a police car a few hundred feet away. A surge of hope and excitement raced through my body as I rushed toward the car, my arms swinging wildly in the air.

"Help! Police!" I shouted.

Officer Bombeck and his partner, Officer Mullins, turned as they heard my disconcerting words. They looked at me and realized my face was somewhat familiar.

"Stone!" shouted Bombeck. "What on earth is going on?"

"Sandra Barton is in trouble," I replied in between breaths. "I think it's the monster!"

"Did you see him?" asked Bombeck, suddenly aroused.

"I saw a black shadow grab her and take her away," I replied, pointing my finger toward the apartment building. "Then I heard her scream from the roof. Hurry, I think her life may be in danger."

I began running back toward the building, the two officers hurrying close behind. When we finally reached the building, we stopped and anxiously looked up toward the roof.

"Sandra Barton!" shouted Bombeck. "This is the police! Please tell us if you're all right!"

There was a moment of silence and then a muffled scream in the distance. Bombeck looked at his partner, and they hurried into the alleyway. When they reached the back of the building, the officers pointed to the fire escape and the three of us began climbing upward. Reaching the roof, Bombeck peered hesitantly over the precipice into the thick darkness. He motioned to Mullins and they grabbed for their guns.

"This is the police!" shouted Bombeck. "Put your arms in the air and surrender!"

We moved slowly onto the roof, the officers' guns poised to fire.

"Police! Halt where you are!"

Failing to receive a reply, we stepped cautiously across the roof.

"Doesn't seem to be anyone here," whispered Bombeck. "Just what the heck is going on, anyway?"

They turned to me. I had followed their footsteps. "They were here, I promise you," I said.

The officers frowned, and glanced at the adjacent rooftops. They were bathed in darkness and utterly silent.

"This is the police!" Bombeck shouted into the darkness. "Surrender immediately!"

The declaration was met with silence. Bombeck glanced at his partner, and they began walking toward the edge of the roof. Looking down toward Central Park, they spotted a figure in black making his way across the avenue. I could see a motionless female body lay draped across his shoulder.

"That must be them!" I said.

"Halt right there!" shouted Bombeck, holding his gun in the air.

"This is the police!"

The demand caused the huge black figure to turn with a snarl, giving us a glimpse of the wild, tufted hair and the wide, hideous mouth. We watched in disbelief as he ignored the command, and kept walking across the street, disappearing inside the park.

Rushing across the roof, the officers clambered back down the fire escape to the street below. I trailed behind, entertaining elaborate thoughts of the front page story I would soon write.

When we reached the park, we hurried inside, rushing into the darkness. We kept running, glancing into the murky shadows that surrounded us, hoping to catch a glimpse of the hulking figure. Hearing cries of desperation up ahead, we kept running through the darkness. He was making his way across the park and we continued to follow. As we got closer to the bright lights of Fifth Avenue, we could hear the sounds of commotion filling the air. Dashing from the park, we spotted a police car parked across from a nearby building and hurried toward it. Two police officers were kneeling behind the car, their guns aimed at the rooftop.

"Did you see him?" asked Bombeck, bending down behind the car.

"We didn't get a look at him," replied one of them. "But he sure rushed up that building. We heard the woman screaming."

"Well, we've been chasing that madman all the way from the west side," Bombeck told him.

I was still making mental notations of all I had seen as I hunched behind the officers.

"How many hostages?" asked one of the officers.

"One, as far as I know," replied Bombeck.

We could hear a multitude of police sirens wailing in the distance.

"How many perps?"

"Just one, but it's the monster, for sure," Bombeck replied.

"Monster?" said the officer. "I thought that was all a bunch of nonsense concocted by the media and a few scared psychos."

Bombeck looked at him and coughed. "Yeah, well, anyway, the madman they think is the monster," he said.

"Is he armed?"

"Can't tell you, but we never heard any shots fired."

The police sirens began to throb in the air, and soon the cars appeared, rushing down the street. As they screeched to a halt, we spotted Sandra Barton standing at the edge of the rooftop.

"Hurry!" she shouted. "He's getting away!"

Bombeck and the other officers charged toward the building, and began climbing the fire escape. When they reached the top, Sandra Barton rushed toward them.

"He escaped," she said anxiously. "He jumped to the next roof."

The officers peered into the darkness. They realized they would have to follow, but it meant jumping to the next rooftop. One of the officers stepped forward, and staring at the nearby rooftop, leaped into the air. He landed on the opposite ledge, slipped momentarily, and scrambled into the shadows. The other officers waited anxiously, squinting into the darkness, and listening for any sounds of a struggle. When the officer appeared once again at the edge of the building, his gun was hanging limply by his side.
"He was horrible," she moaned.

The officer gently patted her back. "Don't worry, miss," he said. "Everything's all right now."

Chapter Three
Officer Bombeck

I'm telling you, I saw what I saw.

But when I told the sergeant, he scoffed. "You've been working too hard," he said. "All this monster talk has affected your brain."

"But I'm telling you," I persisted. "He turned around and snarled at us. I didn't believe my eyes at first. I mean, he was hairy and bent over. I'm telling you, it was a damned monster."

"Bombeck, I hope you're due for a vacation," the sergeant angrily replied. "If you're not, I'm going to recommend you for leave or have you reassigned to desk duty. That's what I think about your so-called monster."

I stared at the frowning sergeant, totally frustrated.

"I don't need a damned vacation," I argued. "I'm telling you that thing is not human. Ask my partner, Officer Mullins, if you don't believe me. He was standing right next to me on top of that building. We ordered that thing to halt and it looked back at us as if it had just been spat up by Hell itself. Never seen anything like it before in my entire life. Just snarled at us, like we were bothering him or something. That poor girl was lying across one of his shoulders like she had seen him up close. I don't blame her at all. I might have fainted myself if I came face to face with that thing with nothing to protect myself."

"Bombeck, you'd better get some sleep," countered the sergeant. "A nice, long rest and don't come back here until you've gotten those crazy ideas about some kind of monster out of your head. The last thing this department needs is one of our own officers running around screaming about some monster. Geez, you sound like those nutjobs we pull off the street."

I was about to continue to plead my case when Lieutenant Bradley suddenly emerged from the nearby stairwell. We could see a sense of concern etched across his face.

"What did the girl say?" asked the sergeant, abruptly turning away from me.

"Not good, not good," replied the lieutenant with a shake of his head. "It seems as if she thinks the guy is some sort of escaped lunatic, possibly an ex-con. We need to check the records of all convicted felons released in the past year, and area mental hospitals. The only positive is that she wasn't raped. He made advances then desisted. We can probably pick him up on molestation and battery charges and hope we nail him later on the murders. Chances are his lawyers are going to make one hell of an insanity plea, as sure as I'm standing here. But that's not our concern. We've got to find him and bring him in."

"Yes, sir," said the sergeant. "I'll put out an APB and assign all available men to areas around the park."

The lieutenant nodded, glanced at me, and walked away, still shaking his head.

"What were you saying, Bombeck?" the sergeant said, turning back toward me. "Now you heard the lieutenant himself. A loony or a con. No monsters, no fairy godmothers, no dragons. Just a lunatic with an attitude. Now get some rest and forget about seeing monsters, you understand?"

I hung my head and sighed. "I guess you're right, sarge," I said. "I must have gotten caught up in the moment. I guess I am pretty tired."

"Happens to the best of them. Now get some rest."

That was the last I wanted to hear about monsters as I headed for the precinct door. Somehow I felt humiliated and confused, seemingly infected by the illogical people I had listened to at the scene of the murders. I wondered if I was getting soft, influenced by the sensational ravings of the media. I decided I would think about it all later, after a good night's sleep.

I pulled at the door, and stepped outside. It was a warm, quiet night, a complete contrast with the excitement I had experienced only a few hours before. As I glanced at the street, I noticed two people, a man and a woman, standing outside the station, gazing in my direction.

"Did you catch the monster yet?" the woman, wearing a purple top and brown slacks, shouted.

I looked at them and wrinkled my brow, an angry scowl emerging across my face. "Why don't you people go home and leave the department alone?" I finally shouted back.

I watched as they began to laugh. "Get away from here before I have the good sense to arrest you," I said.

They probably realized I was in a surly mood, and they began to slowly walk away, still laughing.

"Monsters," I said to myself. "I think maybe I do need a damned vacation."

Getting into my car, I started the engine, and headed for home. It had been a long night, and as I turned onto Broadway, I began to finally relax. Switching on the radio, I began searching for some soothing music, something to make the long trip back home more enjoyable. When I finally found the station I was looking for, I leaned back and sighed. I was listening to the music, attempting to forget the events of the evening when the music suddenly stopped, interrupted by a blaring news report.

"The so-called monster of Central Park struck again last night. Police said he snatched a young woman from in front of her west side apartment and then proceeded to carry her to the top of several buildings. The shaken woman was reportedly unharmed by the long ordeal and was subsequently treated and released from a midtown Manhattan hospital.

Police are still baffled as to the so-called monster's identity, although authorities believe he may be a mental patient who escaped from an area hospital..."

"Baffled?" I sneered. "Damned media, always ready to scare people and sabotage an on-going investigation. I'd like to arrest all of those sons-of-bitches."

I twisted the dial through a barrage of static until I finally reached the sound of a soft melody. I stared through the windshield, began to relax once again and nodded my head rhythmically to the soothing beat, allowing the day to slowly slip into the recesses of my mind. When the song ended, a male voice began to speak.

"In the news today, the alleged murderer known as the monster of Central Park struck again last night, this time grabbing a woman and carrying her to the top of an east side apartment building..."

The report jolted me from a tranquil haze, and I leaned forward and let out an indignant shout. "God damned jackals! Don't these guys have anything better to do than to keep telling people there's a damned monster on the loose?"

I then reached down and pushed a button, instantaneously silencing the annoying report. "I can do without the damned radio, anyway," I mumbled to myself.

Turning onto the Brooklyn Bridge, I slowly began to calm down. I was glad to finally get out of Manhattan, away from the chaos that all the talk of the monster had caused. I stared ahead and began thinking of a quiet, relaxing night with just my wife and maybe a cold glass of beer. I decided I wouldn't think about the monster again until it was time to go back to work later in the day.

The car soared over the Verrazano-Narrows Bridge, bringing me back to Staten Island. The city's smallest borough, famous for its ferry, was home to many police officers since it offered them the chance to own their own homes and escape the suffocating congestion of the other four boroughs. Besides less people and a hint of a more bucolic landscape, the borough was known for its more conservative politics. It had been a haven for pro-British Tories during the Revolutionary War and had voted for the Southern candidate John Breckinridge, instead of Lincoln, in the election of 1860. More recently, it had attempted to secede from New York City itself complaining of a liberal bias and high taxes.

I leaned back and sighed as I approached my small home in the middle of the island. I was soon pushing open the front door and being met by the excited visage of my wife.

"Did you get a look at the monster?" she asked.

I stared at her and frowned. "Now don't you start with me, Edna," I said. "I've had just about enough of all this monster nonsense."

"But I saw it on TV, right there in your precinct."

"Yeah, yeah," I said. "I know, I'm the one who chased him across the park."

"Did you get a look at him?"

"Yeah, he snarled at me."

She looked at me incredulously. "Is it a monster?"

I glanced at her for a moment, about to nod my head, and then suddenly remembered the precinct house and became angry.

"There are no such things as monsters. Don't you know that, Edna? It's just some lunatic running around killing people, that's all."

She looked at me, put her arms around me, and kissed me on the cheek. "I didn't mean anything by it. I just wanted to hear it from you myself."

"It's the damned media," I replied, becoming angry once again. "Putting all those fool ideas into people's heads. They do it to sell papers or get ratings or something. I almost believed it myself. I took a look at that madman and said to myself, 'So that's the monster.' Almost got myself put on desk duty."

"Why don't you come and have a beer?" she said, leading me by the hand. "That will settle your nerves."

I nodded and followed her to the kitchen. "Sit down on the couch and I'll bring it to you," she said. "Why don't you put on the television and relax? Sounds like you've had a hard day."

I turned, and walked to the living room, still upset over the day's events. Sitting down on the couch, I fumbled for the remote control, and turned on the television. There, on the screen, a woman in pink was in the midst of speaking.

"Police believe the so-called monster is responsible for several murders, including the mutilation of the victims' bodies…"

I stared at the screen and couldn't believe I was hearing another news report about the monster. "Oh, geez," I finally groaned.

Turning off the television, I walked past my wife as she entered the room carrying a can of beer. "What's the matter?" she asked. "Don't you want to sit and have your beer?"

"Monsters, that's the matter. All I hear is talk of monsters. I can't take it anymore."

I walked out of the room, and began climbing the stairs.

"Where are you going?" my wife asked.

"To bed! I don't expect to see any monsters in there."

"Don't you want to sit and relax?"

I didn't reply, continuing my trek up the stairs toward the bedroom. When I reached the top of the stairs, I began grumbling to myself.

"Monsters," I said with a shake of my head. It was the last time I ever wanted to hear about it.

Chapter Four
Sandra Barton

I was standing there holding the hand of the man I was in love with and planned to marry when it all began. We were walking through the dim light and the shadows, and then hurried across the wide avenue in a skirl of faint murmur and stirring breeze.

"It's such a beautiful night," I whispered to him, still clutching his hand. "Why don't we walk through the park?"

"The park? At this hour?" Rob replied. "I mean, don't you think it's too dangerous? People have been killed walking through that park at night."

"Oh, it's as safe as any other place in the city," I foolishly said to him. I don't know why I wanted to walk through the park so bad, it just seemed like the romantic thing to do. Still holding his hand, I pulled him towards me, and kissed him gently on the lips. "Besides, there's a lot more we can do in the park than just walk around." I know it was a silly thing to say, but I was trying so hard to convince him to go into the park.

A sly grin spread across Rob's face as he gazed into my eyes, and poised himself for another kiss. I leaned over, kissed him quickly, then laughed, and began running down the pathway that led into Central

Park. Rob watched as I disappeared into the darkness, stumbled forward, and then followed me into the shadows. I knew he couldn't see me. So still laughing, I hurried deeper inside.

I kept running, foolishly imbued with a sense of youthful passion, unconcerned with the possible dangers that lurked inside the park. When I finally halted, I glanced over my shoulder, hoping to see Rob close behind. But the pathway was empty, not a soul standing amid the darkness. I waited a few moments, hoping to see him emerge from the misty shadows, and then finally began rushing back from where I had come.

"Rob?"

There was no answer. The only sound I could hear was the slight rushing of the wind. I looked around, but only noticed the silhouettes of trees glaring through the darkness.

"Rob?"

After a few moments, I saw a shadow dash from behind the trees and rush down the pathway. I was about to scream when the shadow suddenly threw its head back and began laughing. I could see that it was Rob.

I marched up to him, sneering, angrily throwing my arms in the air. "How could you scare me like that?" I shouted.

As he continued to laugh, I made an attempt to hit him, but he put his arms around me, and held me close. "I told you the park was dangerous," he said, kissing me on the lips.

"I thought something happened to you," I said. "Please don't ever do that to me again."

He smiled. "I'm sorry, I just wanted to remind you that we should be careful walking through the park." He then grabbed my hand, and we walked across a patch of grass gently stirring in the moving breeze.

"Let's sit over there," he whispered, pulling me forward past a clump of trees. I remember looking up at the Manhattan sky, and seeing a glare of light obscure the glowing moon.

We walked across the grass, were ready to sit down, when I heard a noise from behind the bushes. I thought it sounded like some sort of animal, but couldn't be sure. Before I could turn around, whatever was creating the sound rushed forward, a darkened form obscured by the night.

I didn't know what to do. Rob then let go of my hand as the figure lunged toward us, throwing me to the ground. I rolled over in the grass, a variety of shouts and groans filling my head, as the sound of a struggle boomed through the air. Then suddenly there was silence. When I finally looked up, I found myself staring into the darkness. I lifted my head, and turned toward where Rob and I had been standing. I could see the clump of trees, but nobody standing near them. Only the gentle breeze disturbed the utter silence.

"Rob?" There was no reply.

Standing up, I felt a sharp pain in my left leg. I limped across the grass, and headed back down the pathway. I shouted Rob's name once again, but again there was no reply. I looked back at the clump of trees, their branches swaying in the cool, drifting breeze. Then I bowed my head, and began to cry.

The next thing I knew there was a police officer standing next to me. I began to calm down as soon as he began speaking.

"It's very important that we get a description of this guy so we can catch him as soon as possible," he was saying.

I wiped my eyes and threw a surprised look. "Guy?" I repeated. "I'm sorry, officer, but that wasn't a guy. It was either an animal or some sort of madman."

The officer looked at me, and remained serious. "I'm sorry, ma'am," he said, "but we need something more specific."

I didn't know what to reply. I mean, I could see by the look in his eyes that he didn't believe what I had told him. "Rob said the park was dangerous," I finally said. "I just didn't want to believe him." The words echoed in my head, and I began crying once again.

The officer stayed calm, and tried to reassure me. "Now everything will be all right, ma'am," he said. "All we need is some sort of description of the guy."

"You keep saying he's a guy," I argued. "But would a guy snarl like an animal before he attacked? No, that wasn't a guy, officer. It was a creature or maybe a madman, something that grabbed Rob and probably has killed him by now. And it's all my fault. Don't you understand? Rob warned me about the park, I just didn't want to listen. It's all my fault."

"Now, ma'am, even if he is a madman, we have a good chance of tracking him down," replied the officer. "They may be capable of the most hideous acts imaginable, but they are still human beings. Experience tells me it won't be any different in this case. Now you may have thought he was a madman, but try to remember, as difficult as it might be, that we are looking for a human being. A crazed human being, maybe, but still a human being."

"Well, I admit it was pretty dark and I didn't see him too clearly, but there wasn't any doubt that he sounded just like an animal."

"Can you describe him to us? I mean, there's always something that stands out."

I thought for a moment, trying to think of something. "Well, I think he was wearing a long, black coat, if that's any help," I said. "I know it sounds weird, but I think he was wearing a coat."

"Not weird at all. Sounds perfectly reasonable. You see? We can already eliminate it being an animal. By your description, he was wearing clothes."

"Yes, maybe you're right," I said, "but it sure sounded like an animal to me. And what about all those monster rumors? Everyone can't be crazy—"

"Oh, now I understand. You had heard about the monster. Now that makes some sense. Naturally, when you saw something come out of the shadows, you just assumed it was the monster." He paused for a moment, evidently pleased with the logic of his reasoning. "Well, Miss Barton, that clears up a lot of things, but let me tell you once again what you saw was no monster. Just a man — a sick man, maybe — but just a man. As soon as you accept that fact, you may be able to tell us what the man looked like. Right now, it's our only chance to catch this guy."

I stayed silent for a moment, reevaluating my original argument. I had been so sure of what I had seen, and yet, the officer's words seemed to make sense.

"I guess it was the first thing I thought of when I saw him jump out of the shadows," I said. "That monster everybody was talking about. He just seemed so real to me, as if someone else's nightmare had suddenly materialized."

"Quite understandable," replied the officer. "You never know what these psychos will do. But we need to know what this guy looks like."

"I don't think I can help you," I said, the tears welling up in my eyes. "I mean, it was so dark and all the noises he made. I'm afraid I was too distracted by everything that was going on."

"Yes, I guess that makes perfect sense. I don't know if I would be able to identify the man either if I was placed in the situation. But you just take your time and think about it. Anything you could come up with would be a help to us." He paused for a moment to look at my face. "Just try to think about it," he repeated reassuringly. "I'm sure you'll remember something eventually."

I didn't know what to think until they found Rob's body a few minutes later lying in the park. They refused to even let me identify the body because they said it had been mutilated. I really couldn't believe Rob had actually been killed. Somehow, I felt as if it were all my fault. I heard talk of the monster as one of the police officers finally told me he would drive me home. I was only too glad to get away from there, the scene in the park haunting my mind.

The next day, the newspapers were filled with stories of "the Monster of Central Park." How could I have been so stupid as to convince Rob to go through the park, I thought to myself. It was as if I had killed him myself. Though I was still very upset about all that happened, I decided to go to work. Although the monster had not been found, there was a lot of talk about him on the television and in the newspapers. I really didn't know what to make of it.

Then while I was coming home one day, I heard someone shouting my name from across the street. I looked and could see it was that newspaper reporter I first saw in the park. I knew his name was Hudge Stone, so I raised my hand.

It was shortly thereafter that something grabbed me from behind. I could hear his heavy panting in my ears, sounding much like an animal. I was so stunned, I didn't even scream for help. My first thought was that it was the monster. I just couldn't believe it, though. I mean, I couldn't understand what he wanted from me. And then I thought about Rob, and all my fears and sorrows came rushing over me. "Who are you?" I screamed.

He didn't answer. He just kept panting and grunting, carrying me to the apartment building fire escape. He then began climbing up. When we reached the sixth floor, I couldn't take anymore. I looked down, and became so fearful that he was going to drop me that I blacked out.

When I regained consciousness, we were running through the park. This was my chance, I thought to myself. I tried wriggling out of his arms, but he held me tight.

"Who are you?" I screamed once again.

It was then we began climbing up another apartment building. I could see the police cars moaning down below. It was all like a dream. I expected to wake up in own bed any minute. We then reached the roof, and he finally put me down. I immediately ran to the other side of the roof, screaming as loud as I could.

In all the time I was with him, I never really got a very good look at him. I know he was very hairy, and had that dank odor of an animal in the zoo, but I never did get a clear look at his face. He was panting and grunting the whole way. His teeth seemed long and sharp. I don't know what he was. I thought maybe a madman, or maybe a wanted fugitive, but something told me these initial thoughts were incorrect. Maybe he was a monster, although I know that is hard to believe. I mean, monsters aren't supposed to exist. But how can anyone explain what this thing was? A man?

Anyway, before I had a chance to try to talk to him, he leaped to the next rooftop.

"Hurry!" I shouted to the police. "He's getting away!"

The police arrived sometime later. But it was too late. Whatever it was, it had escaped.

The only thing I could think of saying to them was, "He was horrible." I mean, I still didn't know what the hell it was, and in some way, I really didn't want to know.

Chapter Five
New York Herald

BIGFOOT IN THE BIG APPLE?

By Hudge Stone

People who claimed to have seen the so-called "Monster of Central Park" say he looks very much like the legendary Bigfoot, although police officials discount the reports.

No one knows who or what "the Monster of Central Park" is, although he is thought to be responsible for several murders in and around the Central Park area in New York City.

"He looked very much like Bigfoot," claimed one eyewitness. "He was definitely a hairy, ape-like creature."

The existence of Bigfoot, or Sasquatch as he is also known, has always been disputed by most mainstream scientists as being mythology, folklore, misidentification, or hoaxes. Most Bigfoot sightings have occurred in remote areas of the United States with the creature being reported in the forests of the Northeast and South. The most common sightings have been in the Pacific Northwest.

If one of the creatures is currently living in or around the Central Park area, experts say the mystery will soon be solved.

"There is no way he can escape capture in New York City," said one anthropologist. "If it is Sasquatch, we will know very soon."

Police officials, however, remain skeptical. "As we've been saying over and over again, the perp is a male human being," said a police spokesman. "All this talk of monsters and Bigfoot does nothing to help this very real on-going investigation."

According to eyewitness accounts, Bigfoot is a large, ape-like bipedal creature with broad shoulders and a strong build. Except for the face, hands and feet, most of the body is covered with short, shaggy black or dark brown hair. Enormous human-like footprints give the creature its name.

Many New Yorkers who claim to have seen "the Monster of Central Park," say he is large and ape-like with black hair covering a large portion of his body.

According to one anthropologist, Sasquatch or Bigfoot is "omnivorous." He is further described as an "opportunistic carnivore."

The bodies found in New York during the past week have been missing part or all of their brain matter. Many people feel this is a sign that "the Monster of Central Park" is a creature rather than a human being.

According to eyewitnesses, including Sandra Barton, the woman abducted, "the Monster of Central Park" may be a madman, escaped convict, or a creature of some sort.

Describing the "monster," Barton simply said, "He was horrible."

Along with the Loch Ness Monster and Yeti, Bigfoot is probably the most famous creature in cryptozoology, the study of rumored animals that may or may not exist.

Although reports of a large, hairy, ape-like "wild man" date back to the late 18th century, accounts of the modern Bigfoot began in 1958 with enormous footprints reported in Humboldt County, California.

Evidence is currently lacking to prove the existence of Sasquatch, although many academics and professionals welcome further research and acknowledge there is a possibility that the creature may exist.

Even if the reports of Bigfoot are discounted, one thing is certain: there is something running around the streets of Manhattan abducting women and killing people.

-END-

Chapter Six
Doctor Luther Steele

"Plagued by petty jealousies and the constant need for approval, prone to horrendous acts of violence against even his own kind and irrational hatreds based upon superstition and selfishness, and always tending toward oppression, whether it be to vanquish his perceived adversaries, or dominate his most profound affections, is not the human creature a savage beast at heart?"

My eyes stayed riveted on the crowd before me, as I launched my arms into the air with a fervent urgency that accentuated my bold and ominous words. Then I paused and leaned forward, gazing from the lectern to the attentive audience below.

"What was the first thing our primitive ancestors did with the knowledge they had gradually obtained? Why, they used it to more efficiently exterminate each other! The first inventors of pebble tools, the African Australopithecines, immediately used the new weapon to kill members of their own species. When Peking Man learned to preserve fire, the mutilated and charred bones of his species were found among the cinders. This inexorable tendency toward murder is the legacy of human history. Even early fossil human skulls, dated before Cro-Magnon times, repeatedly display puncture marks, probably caused by sharp objects. The Cro-Magnons themselves left behind innumerable fossils that clearly show a propensity to murder each other.

"Why, even our Bible tells us of our murderous origins. Lest we not forget, we are the progeny of Cain! So what has changed in the centuries that have passed? Not much, my friends, just the clothing and the methods. For you see, we are still the killer ape at heart. We have only become more cunning and inventive in accordance with the development of laws and customs. But underneath our clothing, we are still the savage beast who roamed the earth all those centuries ago."

I paused for a moment so my words could sink in. I stared down at the crowd with a threatening look, and then continued my dissertation.

"My fellow scientists, we are the beings with the supposedly superior brains, and yet our history is saturated with countless acts of violence in the name of money, country, and religion. Progress to us is the quest for a more efficient machine, whether it is used to obliterate, or increase our production of items in the hope of generating greater quantities of money. It is the progress of the machine that has been the focus of human history, not the progress of the human being.

"Human behavior, as it relates to his psychological relation to society, has actually deteriorated. His value to society has always been founded upon his ability to make money or in assisting the efficiency of the machine, not in his ability to improve human thought and behavior. We have been duped to believe that convenience necessarily leads to human progress, but that, of course, is the philosophy of those shackled to materialism. I say to you, human progress can only be attained through the improvement of the human brain, and, thus, human society. But what do we know of the human brain?

"Psychology in our society is based upon materialism and medications, not the mental ingredients necessary for human contentment. Do we know how the brain assimilates memories, experience, and information in order to formulate judgments of motives and desire? Do we realize an understanding of the human brain can unlock the mysteries of illness and behavior, or are we satisfied with inconclusive theories created in the name of ego and profit? The human brain, ladies and gentlemen, that should be the goal of our continuous research, for that alone can help effectuate a new era in furthering human progress."

My solemn words were punctuated by animated arm gestures and fascinating facial expressions. It was as if I were speaking from the pulpit, articulating a gospel of scientific inquiry and abstract ideology. I looked down at my notes, preparing to continue the discourse, when I heard the faint sound of grunting coming from the wings of the stage. I looked over and was startled by the sight of a huge, hulking shadow. As I squinted into the darkness, the figure began grunting once again in short, rapid bursts, as if he were attempting to impart a sense of panic. I listened calmly to the nervous discharge and frowned.

"Ngila! Ngila!" I began to whisper sternly, trying not to disturb the attentive audience below.

Upon hearing the words, the figure fell silent, and then as quietly as he appeared, vanished into the shadows. I remained staring at the spot I had first seen the figure for a few moments, and then satisfied he was gone, turned back toward my confused colleagues.

"Please excuse this unexpected disturbance," I said. "It was an assistant of mine, quite indifferent to the proceedings of this great body. A momentary dilemma to him is always of great importance, and he thinks nothing of interrupting the most momentous occasion to inform me of his constant bewilderment. You may wonder why I do not discharge such a seeming impediment and yet, he provides reliable assistance to me once the alleged crisis has passed. I hate to think if there ever was a genuine problem, for I do not think I would heed his warnings. Then again, it is better to be too cautious than utterly careless in the process of research and scientific exploration. On this, I know my esteemed colleagues will agree. For it is intense and verified research that is the key to our search for a healthier and more cooperative human being. That, I trust, is the goal of every individual sitting inside this room today. I know most of you are familiar with Biocea Systems and our continued efforts to eradicate disease and improve the human mind. We have obtained a number of successful results through the years and hope to achieve more in the near future. I hope I can rely on your continued support."

A surge of enthusiastic applause filled the room as I nodded, turned, and walked from the lectern. I was immediately greeted by a contingent of scientific colleagues from across the country. They smiled and shook my hand with firm approval. I attempted to reciprocate, but not being a man easily disposed to smiling, simply nodded my head a few times in an appreciative manner.

"Fine speech, doctor," said one of them. "But we were eager to hear the results of your most recent studies."

"Sorry, gentlemen," I replied. "The research we are currently working on is not yet completed. I tried to give my esteemed colleagues an idea of the direction we're taking, and as soon as we're prepared to publish the results, I would be more than happy to provide the details. I should think, if we are successful, an extensive demonstration might even be in order."

"I'm sure it would be most enlightening. I assume it has something to do with your previous studies on behavioral abnormalities."

I nodded hesitantly. "Yes, you are most astute, professor, but as I said, I really cannot go into any details at the present time. The studies are currently in progress and I fear jeopardizing, in any way, a most objective assessment of our eventual findings."

"Yes, yes, of course," said one of the men. "We only hope you will return to discuss at length your published results."

"Most certainly," I said. "Now if you gentlemen will excuse me, I fear I have urgent business at hand. Although my assistant is hasty in his alarm, I do not think he would interrupt my speech without sufficient justification."

The men nodded in agreement and began to applaud once again as I uttered a cordial farewell. They watched as I walked toward the wings of the stage, and disappeared into the shadows.

Moments later, a side door opened amid a burst of sunlight, and I emerged onto the streets of New York City. Once outside, I hurriedly made my way to the parking lot where I retrieved my car, and pulled out into the avenue. I slowly drove to a nearby alleyway where I suddenly halted, peering into the blue-gray shadows. Leaning over, I rolled down the window and began to shout into the darkened gap.

"Ngila! Ngila!"

After a few moments, the hulking figure in the long, black coat appeared. He hesitantly moved into the light, and then dashed toward the waiting car.

Chapter Seven
Ngila

Believe in God. Believe. Doctor says he will bring me to the church sometime. He says he wants to see what the people think of me.

"Same as them," I said to him. "A man."

Doctor was smiling. He does not smile very much. "I wonder how they would react to that statement," he said.

I didn't know what he meant. Then the doctor's mate came into the room. Her name is Catherine.

"Hello, my dear," said the doctor. "Ngila and I have just been discussing God."

"Very interesting," she said. "And what did Ngila have to say?"

"Believe in God. Believe."

"That is good," she said. "But you must live by His principles."

I looked at her, and then at the doctor.

"Yes, Ngila," he said. "There is no room for hypocrisy in religion."

Do not know the meaning of that word, but Catherine was angry.

"Please, Luther, I'm trying to be serious," she said. "Ngila must learn that all human beings must be responsible for their actions."

"Yes, yes, but despite that, we have made great progress, my dear," the doctor said. "Why, think of it, only a few years ago Ngila could speak no English and had no idea what it meant to be a man in a civilized society."

She looked at me. "That is true," she said. "But there is much work to be done."

"Yes, but our most current problem is that Ngila has said he desires to mate again," the doctor said. "What I'm trying to say is, Ngila has found another woman."

Catherine now angry again. "Put an end to it, Luther," she said. "Ngila has done enough mating for the time being."

"I don't think I can," the doctor said. "I mean, it's all part of his education."

Yes, education. Mate. Live. Hunt. Yes, Ngila is a man. A man. Believe in God. Believe.

Chapter Eight
Hudge Stone

The days passed, many doubting the murderer would ever be apprehended, and soon, the story was relegated to the list of unsolved crimes in the vast, teeming city. I was one of the few who had refused to give up hope of finding the mysterious killer, was confident a new lead would turn up, or the killer, whoever he was, would be foolish enough to attempt another murder.

Nothing had occurred the past few nights, and so, as I sat down at my desk, it was with a hint of resignation. It was then I noticed the large, white envelope sitting there on the desk, a Washington, D.C. address printed at the top. I studied the envelope for a moment, wondering what it possibly could contain, and then tore it open. Inside were several papers from the National Genome Project, a government program coordinated by the U.S. Department of Energy and the National Institutes of Health. The goal of the project was to identify all the genes in human DNA and then determine the sequences of the three billion chemical bases that comprise the human genetic code. I glanced at the pages, noticing they contained information about the extensive project, including its research goals, its potential benefits, and the ethical, legal, and social issues involved.

"A genome is all the DNA in an organism, including its genes,"

I read. "Genes carry information for producing all the proteins required by all organisms. These proteins determine, among other things, how the organism looks, how well its body metabolizes food or fights infection, and even how it behaves."

In the margin of the page was a handwritten message. It included the words, "call me," and a local telephone number. I stared at the page for a few moments, trying to figure out what it had to do with any of the stories I had worked on. I then wondered why it wasn't sent to one of the paper's science reporters, and thought that maybe some mistake had been made.

I read the handwritten message once again. "Call me," it said. I wondered who might have sent it, and decided I would try dialing the number. After several rings, a deep voice answered on the other end.

"Hello?"

"Hello, this is Hudge Stone of the *Herald*, do you work for the National Genome Project?"

There was a pause on the other end. "Stone, yes, oh, yes, I'm the one who sent you those papers. The name's Doctor Lido."

"Are you with the government?"

"I can't tell you that right now. My job may be in jeopardy. But it's very important that you investigate that program."

"Where do I begin?" I asked.

"Well, I'll meet with you and give you what I've got. That should start you off in the right direction."

"Does this have anything to do with the monster story?"

"It might." He paused for a moment. "Well, I can tell you it involves a Doctor Steele, who is very much associated with the story you're working on. But that's all I can say over the phone. I fear I've said too much already. The phones here may be bugged, you know. Anyway, I think it would be well worth your trouble if you met me in Bryant Park. Before there's any more bloodshed."

My heart was racing, the adrenaline flooding my system. "I'll be there, doctor," I replied.

"Good, all it's going to take is a little digging, which should be right up your alley. Are you intrigued?"

"Sure, I'm interested, but can't you tell me any more about how it relates to the monster story?"

"Meet me in Bryant Park. I'll be there in an hour. I'll wait ten minutes, and if you don't show up, I'll expect another call from you. Do you understand?"

"Don't worry, I'll be there," I said, my face close against the receiver.

I placed the phone down, sat back, and exhaled, beads of sweat clinging to my forehead. There was a strange sensation in my stomach — a gut feeling that it was something big. I walked over to my city editor, and began telling him about the conversation I had just had. My editor looked at me and nodded.

I was soon on a subway train headed for Bryant Park. The park was located behind the New York Public Library, an area nestled on the corner of West Forty-second Street and Avenue of the Americas. I walked slowly toward the park, knowing Doctor Lido was not due to arrive for another few minutes. It was a cool day, the pale rays of the sun slanting through some dark clouds that had scudded in from the north, sending a drifting breeze wandering down the avenue.

As I made my way inside the park, I immediately noticed a balding man in a tan raincoat standing by himself. He was holding a black attaché case and, undoubtedly, waiting for someone. Although he was early, I was sure it was Doctor Lido. Turning on the small tape recorder in my pocket, I approached.

"Doctor Lido?"

The man smiled, and extended his hand. "Yes, that's right. Are you Stone?"

"Nice to meet you, doctor," I replied, shaking his hand. "What have you got for me on this government project?"

"Right to the point, Stone, I like that. First, let me tell you most of the information I'm going to give you is confidential. You'll have to verify it on your own without using my name. Do you understand? No names. I'd like to expose Doctor Steele's insidious study, but I really don't want to lose my job doing it. If you mention me to anyone, I'll deny ever speaking to you."

I nodded. "Don't worry, doctor, I know how to protect my sources. The only thing I can give you is my word, and if you trust me, I won't disappoint you. All I ask is that you tell me the truth."

"Fair enough, Stone. What I'm about to give you is information pertaining to the government program known as the National Genome Project. For you own information, I'm a research scientist with the government who happened to get involved in the project soon after its commencement. You see, an intense competition developed between the government and private companies in an attempt to map the human genes. One of those companies, Biocea Systems, is headed by a Doctor Luther Steele."

"But I thought the genetic information is available to the public?"

"It is, as far as the government is concerned. All of our genetic data is available on the Internet. I only wish these private companies were compelled to do the same. You see, America and Great Britain have already agreed to share genetic data, including the human DNA sequence and its variations, with scientists everywhere. Private companies like Biocea, however, have refused to cooperate."

"But have any laws been broken? I mean, what is the severity of the possible crime involved?"

"Well, to begin with, murder. After that, I think you're going to have to find out for yourself and then decide. Maybe you'll be able to speak with Doctor Dekko Quant some time during your inquiry. He's one of the directors of the government program and a leading authority on genetic engineering. That's the best I can do for you right now."

"Where can I find Doctor Quant?"

"He works in Washington, but he's very hard to get in touch with. I must urge you to find out everything you can about the project before you attempt to speak with him. It's very important that you know what to ask. That is, if you can reach him at all."

Doctor Lido opened his case and pulled a sheaf of papers from inside. He handed the bundle to me.

"Here are some of the documents concerning the project," he said. "I suggest you read them very carefully. You can call me again when you're ready to proceed."

I nodded.

"Good luck, Stone, and be careful. These private companies are very protective of their work." Doctor Lido closed his case, and began walking away without looking back. I watched him until he finally disappeared around a corner. I cradled the papers against my body, and began walking back toward Fifth Avenue.

Hailing a cab at the corner, I decided I would go back to my apartment and read the papers there. The last thing I wanted was to lead any interlopers back to where I worked. I placed the papers on my lap, glancing at the title page. It was stamped, "National Genome Project," and included a basic introduction of the program's goals. I slipped the papers inside my briefcase and looked up, wondering if the cab driver had seen what I was doing. If Doctor Lido was correct, no one could be trusted until the story was finally completed.

The cab pulled up to the curb, and I stepped out still clutching my briefcase. I hurried past the door of my apartment building, walked across the lobby floor, and then slipped inside an empty elevator. I was anxious to begin reading the papers Doctor Lido had given me, and resolved not to leave my room until I had finished. Stepping out of the elevator, I walked to my apartment, opened the door, and disappeared inside. Walking to the bedroom, I placed the briefcase on the bed, opened it, and retrieved the thick stack. I looked once again at the title page, and then slid upon the bed. Lying back on a couple of pillows, I began reading.

"Knowledge of DNA variations among individuals can lead to revolutionary new ways to diagnose, treat, and hopefully, prevent thousands of disorders," the papers began. "To help achieve these goals, the National Genome Project hopes to store this information in databases, develop tools for data analysis, and establish a dialogue between the public and scientists that helps produce informed decisions in utilizing these advances and prevent their abuse."

I read the words and wondered what possibly could have gone wrong with the government program. I began flipping through the pages, trying to figure out where it was leading, what possible error had been made, and how Doctor Steele was involved. In the middle of the report were some charts that were labeled, "Human DNA Levels." I glanced at them, still confused as to their pertinence, and moved on. As I neared the report's conclusion, the phone rang.

"This is Stone," I said, fumbling with the receiver.

"Yes, Mr. Stone, this is the lobby. There's a Doctor Lido here who says he would like to speak with you."

I thought for a moment, wondering what Doctor Lido was doing in my lobby, what he had forgotten to tell me. He was a valuable source, the most valuable source I had at the present time, and probably had some valuable information that would make the whole pile of papers actually make some sense.

"Okay, send him up," I finally replied.

I placed the receiver down and sighed. A reporter never knew what an anonymous source was capable of doing. That's why they were so frowned upon by the paper's editors. I, however, knew that without Doctor Lido I would never have a chance of uncovering the story. I had always believed anonymous sources were valuable as long as the information they provided could be substantiated by other officials who were willing to be quoted "on the record." I knew editors hated the idea of giving anyone anonymity because it allowed the source to tell the reporter anything without having to take any responsibility. But if a story was important enough, I was willing to take the risk.

After a few moments, I heard someone knocking at the door. I walked over, and began opening the door, when I noticed a tall man in a black suit and sunglasses standing in the doorway. The thought of danger sped through my mind as I instinctively attempted to shut the door, but it was too late.

I felt a powerful leg on the other side of the door kick it open as I stumbled backwards. Then I watched as the man grabbed something from beneath his jacket. Before I could react, the man struck me, and I slumped to the floor. I could see the man walking toward the bedroom as an enveloping haze invaded my head. Then I remembered the National Genome papers. I lay there thinking about moving, thinking about preventing the theft of the papers, and then realized there was nothing I could do to hinder the man's actions. I felt my eyes close, my body becoming relaxed, and then suddenly, I fell unconscious.

When I opened my eyes again, my head was killing me. Getting up and still rubbing my head, I walked to the bedroom. After a thorough search, I realized the only things missing from the apartment were the papers detailing the government project.

I lay down on the bed and realized I had spent most of the day in a lethargic stupor. Then I wondered whether I would ever be able to get in touch with Doctor Lido again. As I thought more about it, it seemed imperative that I get up and resume the investigation as soon as possible. Apparently, there was something about the genome project that had gone terribly wrong, although not knowing that piece of information probably saved my life. That, however, would not deter me from continuing the investigation. In fact, I was more determined than ever to find out what that missing piece of information was.

Swinging my legs over the side of the bed, I slid to the floor, attempting to suppress an agonizing groan. I was still somewhat dazed, but I knew I had to try to contact Doctor Lido as soon as possible, wondering if the attack and theft would have any affect on his willingness to continue talking to me. Even with anonymity, the doctor's life may be in danger. But I knew I had to try to convince him to continue supplying information if I ever was to finally learn the truth about the monster. Of course, there was Doctor Quant, but there still wasn't any way to get in touch with him, and even if there was, I wondered if the doctor would speak with me.

Picking up the phone, I began dialing Doctor Lido's number. After a few tense moments and several rings, I was relieved when I heard the familiar deep voice.

"Hello, who's calling?"

"Doctor Lido, this is Hudge Stone."

"Stone? Are you all right?"

"I'm fine, doctor, but the genome papers have been stolen. They came to my apartment and took everything you gave me. I was hoping you'd still be willing to talk."

"Are you sure you want to continue the investigation, Stone? Things seem to have gotten a little too dangerous. How far did you get in the papers I gave you?"

"Unfortunately, not very far. I only read the first few pages. Somehow, they knew what I was doing. Apparently, they didn't want me to read any further."

"That's what I was afraid of. Once you know about the project, you'll inform the rest of the world, and they don't want that to happen. Does anybody know you're calling me?"

"I don't think so. Can we meet somewhere again?"

"Listen, Stone, there's a little restaurant on the Upper East Side. We'll be able to talk there without any fear. Meet me there in two hours."

I listened to the directions, placed the phone down, and sighed. At least, Doctor Lido had agreed to see me again. Grabbing a light jacket, I rushed out of the apartment, and made my way downstairs. I was soon standing outside my apartment building, searching for a cab.

Amid a glaring sun, a cab soon pulled up to the curb, and I got inside. As it sped away, I glanced out the rear window, but couldn't tell if anyone was attempting to follow. The cab halted a few minutes later, and I slid out of the back seat, still looking behind me. The street was rather deserted; a good sign as far as I was concerned, and somewhat relieved, stepped inside the tiny restaurant.

"Stone," I heard a voice whisper from the other side of the room.

The restaurant was dark and empty, still awaiting the surge of the dinnertime crowd. I could see a few patrons sitting at the bar, apparently intent on forgetting the rest of the day as soon as possible. I slowly walked past them until I spotted Doctor Lido sitting at a table near the back.

"It's good to see you again," I said.

Doctor Lido motioned for me to sit down. "And I see you're up and about. I want to tell you I respect you very much for wanting to continue the investigation. Most men would have given up rather easily. Did I understand you correctly, they took all of the papers?"

I nodded.

"Well, at least you know something now about the project. I think maybe it's time you had a talk with Doctor Quant. As you know, he was one of the directors of the project. He wanted you to know everything you could about it before speaking with him. I guess I'll have to explain what happened. I'm sure he'll understand."

"Does he know anything about this Doctor Steele you were talking about?"

"You'd know if only you had the chance to read all of the papers," replied Doctor Lido. "He became a staunch critic of Doctor Steele and Biocea after learning of their proposed study."

"And what study is that?"

"Let's just say Doctor Quant came to believe some of Doctor Steele's studies were an unnecessary intrusion and violated the sanctity of life. He began to argue constantly with him until he finally decided the world must know about what Doctor Steele was doing."

"Maybe I should speak with Doctor Steele."

Doctor Lido frowned. "Eventually, but first let me arrange for you to talk to Doctor Quant. He is apt to provide you with an infinitely more objective assessment than our friend, Doctor Steele. I'll get in touch with you after the interview has been arranged. Don't tell anyone, including your editors, about the interview until after it has taken place. Do you understand?"

"I won't tell a soul, doctor. Only I hope I can do the interview as soon as possible."

Doctor Lido nodded. "I will try," he said with a smile. "Doctor Quant is a very busy man. Now I suggest you go back and get some rest. I doubt they'll bother coming after you again."

I watched as Doctor Lido stood up, and began putting on his tan raincoat and black hat. I then followed him outside.

"Get some rest," repeated the doctor. He then turned, and began walking away. He had only taken a few steps when a man, wearing a dark suit and sunglasses, appeared from across the street. The man bumped into Doctor Lido and then reached inside his suit jacket. I could see the man's hand emerge clutching a gun with a silencer. There was a muffled shot and then Doctor Lido collapsed to the ground.

Instinctively, I leaped toward the man. I pushed him to the sidewalk, knocking the gun from his hand, and then tried to recover the weapon. There was a mad scramble, and when I realized the man would reach the gun first, darted into a nearby alleyway. I hurried down the narrow corridor until I reached an intersection, turned to my left, and followed another corridor into the dark, gray shadows.

I continued running down the corridor until I glimpsed the sunlight peeking into the alleyway from the open street. Deciding I would stay in this shadowy labyrinth, I turned around and headed back to the intersection. There was no sign of anyone following me, but I dared not remain in one spot for very long. Turning into another corridor, one filled with windows and steel fire escapes, a thought came to me. I decided I would climb to the roof of one of the buildings and remain there until it was safe.

I clambered up the winding steel staircase as quietly as possible. At each landing, I peered into the shadows, wondering if Doctor Lido's murderer was still attempting to find me. When I finally reached the roof, I looked down over the precipice and could see the man in the dark suit hurrying down below. I silently stepped backwards onto the roof until I could no longer be seen from below. I had only taken a few steps when I felt something soft against my back. Turning around, I stared up into the face of the monster.

My face stiffened in surprise. My jaw dropped and my eyes opened wide, until they were about to burst from the sockets. I stood staring at the massive half-bent figure before me, dwarfed by the large bulging shoulders and thick neck supporting a skull covered with thick tufts of unruly hair, unable to even cry out in fear. I looked at the monster's face, the high eyebrow-ridges, the broad nose, and large flat forehead, and now understood why Sandra Barton had described him as looking like an escaped madman.

The monster looked back at me for a moment, his eyes glaring from beneath the protruding eyebrow-ridges. "Doctor want to see you," he finally said in a low, guttural grunt.

"Doctor?" I gasped. "What doctor?"

"You will come with me," the monster replied, draping his arms around my body.

Still speechless, I felt myself rising into the air. Held tight against the monster's body, I watched in bewilderment as we bounded across the rooftop. When we reached the edge of the roof, the monster leaped into the air, and landed on the adjoining rooftop. We traveled in this way for several minutes, the gargantuan mass of Manhattan skyscrapers glistening in the distance. I closed my eyes, dizzy and frightened, and then everything fell away into placid darkness.

Chapter Nine
The Human Genome Project

The Human Genome Project, completed in April of 2003, was the international, collaborative research program whose goal was the complete mapping of the genetic blueprint for building a human being.

The $3 billion project determined the sequence or exact order of nearly all of the 3 billion-plus chemical building blocks that constitute the human DNA code. The human genome contains these deoxyribonucleic acid base pairs in the 23 pairs of chromosomes within the nucleus of our cells. Each chromosome contains hundreds to thousands of genes, which carry the instructions for making proteins.

The project found that human beings contain 20,000 to 25,000 genes, or about the same number it takes to make a small flowering plant or a tiny worm.

The genes in the sequences of these DNA building blocks are like letters that create words. The completed sequence of the human genome is similar to having all the pages of a manual needed to make the human body. The problem now is how to read all these pages and understand how all the parts work together.

It is expected that genome-based research will eventually lead to the development of highly effective diagnostic tools, to the understanding of health needs based on a person's individual genetic make-up, and to designing new and better treatments for disease.

The goal is individualized analysis of a person's genome leading to preventive medicines and an understanding of risks of future illness. Changes in medical science based on the completed genome are still about ten to fifteen years away.

Companies, however, have already begun offering genetic tests that can show if one is predisposed to illnesses such as breast cancer, blood clotting, cystic fibrosis, liver diseases, and many others. Scientists can now narrow down a search on a disease to a particular gene.

Another benefit is the analysis of similarities between DNA sequences from different organisms to construct an in-depth study of evolution. It is expected that many evolutionary questions can be found on the molecular level, and will be part of the study of molecular biology.

The question of who owns the human genome is still open to debate. Although the sequencing by the Human Genome Project was made public, private companies have filed thousands of patents on human genes. Most of these patent applications have not been acted upon, so it's still not known how much of the genome can be used for commercial purposes.

The idea of beginning a coordinated study of the human genome arose from a series of scientific conferences held between 1985 and 1987. The Human Genome Project then began in 1990 with funding from the National Institutes of Health and the Department of Energy.

Nations having human genome research programs as part of the collaboration included the United Kingdom, France, Germany, China, and Japan. A privately funded biotechnology company used its own technique in putting together the sequence of the human genome.

The first phase of the project — with a draft of the human genome being published in separate journals — was completed in February of 2001. The final sequencing was then completed in April of 2003.

Chapter Ten
Hudge Stone

The whir of computers throbbed through the air as I awoke from my impromptu slumber. I looked up and found myself sitting inside a huge room, unusually cool from the continuous air conditioning, the nearby computers in the midst of analyzing unknown information. I glanced across the room and could see glass-enclosed robots, the size of small cars, resolutely going about their work.

"Please make yourself at home," said a voice a few feet away.

Still in a daze, I recoiled at the sound of the voice. I glanced to my right, and saw a man in a white medical gown, with gleaming white hair, standing across the room.

"Don't get up," said the man. "There isn't any need for formality here. I'm Doctor Luther Steele, and you, I imagine, are Mr. Stone."

"Doctor Steele?" I repeated. "So then the monster is part of one of your studies."

"I see our friend, Doctor Lido, told you more than he should have," said the doctor, walking across the room.

I blinked my eyes, attempting to emerge from the haze enveloping my head. "But what about your genome study, doctor?"

Doctor Steele looked at me and grimaced. "What is it you want, Stone?" he finally asked. "Money? Is that it?"

The question startled me. "I don't want your money, doctor," I replied. "I was only trying to discover the truth. Who exactly is that monster roaming the streets of the city?"

"Is that all you desire, Mr. Stone?"

I nodded. "Is he part of some genome study?"

"You know nothing about Ngila!" Doctor Steele shouted back. He made the statement in such a threatening tone of voice that I slid back in my seat as if preparing to be struck. "So you want to know about Ngila? A very interesting story, I must say. I guess you realized as much from what that meddling doctor told you."

"Apparently, Doctor Lido thought it was important enough to sacrifice his life."

"And that did not dissuade you from abandoning this whole sordid affair? I imagined you were much smarter than that, Mr. Stone."

"People are dying out there," I replied. "They have a right to know what the hell is going on."

"You sound like an idealist, Mr. Stone. Well, that's fine by me. I, too, was once an idealist. You might say this whole experiment was founded upon the idealistic desire for a better world. But, then, you see, one must take note of reality every now and then."

"Like murder?"

"You don't understand, do you, my friend? You fail to comprehend the utter importance of the experiments we were undertaking. Someone like Ngila is one in a million. Why, my God, you only have to listen to him speak English. The implications are astounding."

"Just who is Ngila?"

"That, my friend, is not so easy to answer. I must start at the beginning and tell you everything that has occurred for you to decide for yourself. Then, maybe, you'll understand how valuable Ngila is."

"I'm listening, doctor." I watched as Doctor Steele prepared to speak. His gestures suddenly became quire animated, and as he began telling his story, I could detect a certain passion swelling in his eyes.

"You see, we started with the common human gut bacterium *Escherichia coli*; the fruit fly, known scientifically as Drosophila melanogaster, and the laboratory mouse. Did you know the fruit fly cell has only 13,600 genes compared to a human's 25,000? Well, it's true, and almost ninety percent of the genes between a fruit fly and a human are similar. That's why it was so important to decipher these nonhuman organisms first."

"What did you find?"

"Well, with the help of our computers, we began piecing together the genetic sequences that constitute DNA. Then we began to determine what the function of each of the genes was and how they interacted with each other. Next, we began working on the mouse genome, more than a billion pairs of the nucleotide compounds that constitute its DNA. But, you see, sequencing, or establishing the order of the nucleotides, is only the first step to understanding a genome."

"How does it work, doctor?"

"Well, first, the DNA is extracted, either mitochondrial or nuclear DNA, depending upon whether it is taken from the mitochondria of the cell body or from the cell nucleus. The mitochondrial DNA, used to reconstruct generations utilizing maternal relatives, is inherited solely from the mother, while the nuclear DNA, which retraces families through the father and mother, is inherited from both parents, and is unique to every individual except identical twins.

"The DNA is then divided down the center like a zipper, and only one half of the zipper is used. The trick is recreating the other half of the zipper, and discovering the sequence of the bases. The bases, adenine, guanine, cytosine, and thymine, are abbreviated A, G, C, and T. When reconstructing DNA, bases A and T always bind together, as well as bases C and G.

"We begin by placing one half of the DNA strand in a test tube with some free bases and an enzyme that causes the free bases to attach to the strand, thereby recreating the zipper. Modified bases are then added to mark the location of a base on the zipper. The process includes the reconstruction of thousands of strands in each test tube."

"Was the same process used on the human genome?" I asked.

"Exactly," replied the doctor. "We began with chromosomes 5, 16, 19, 21 and 22, and found vital information about disease, various cancers, hypertension and diabetes. As you know, there are twenty-three pairs of chromosomes in the human genome that consist of coiled strands of DNA. Different arrangements of the base pairs inside the DNA molecule constitute the code for the human gene. The genes form the blueprint for the proteins that dictate the function of cells.

"For example, chromosome 22 contains over five hundred genes that play a role in an estimated thirty-five diseases, including some cancers, schizophrenia, deafness and heart ailments. The genes also include eye color, hair color, height, and all of the inherited traits that make us unique from each other and from other creatures. Chromosome 21, which contains over two hundred genes, was found to include Down syndrome, epilepsy, Lou Gehrig's disease and Alzheimer's."

"Then what exactly went wrong with the genome study?" I asked.

Doctor Steele looked at me, a strange gleam in his eyes. "Why, nothing went wrong with the genome study, Mr. Stone. In fact, it is going so well we are learning something new every day."

"But what about Ngila?"

"He is part of one of our most ambitious studies, Mr. Stone," replied the doctor. "One in which we will learn more about the human being than in any previous study. You see, we plan on discovering mutations in entire lineages, the migration habits of various population groups based upon the genetic material in their mitochondrial DNA, and the mutations of the Y chromosome through time thereby tracing the lineage and migration of the male population."

"Ngila is going to help you discover all that? But he is a cold-blooded killer, doctor."

"That I find hard to believe, Mr. Stone."

"But there are bodies."

"You don't understand, Mr. Stone. Ngila knows nothing of the laws of a civilized society. He is from another part of the world, an innocent soul who obeys only the laws of nature."

As the words fell from Doctor Steele's mouth, there was a sudden noise, a tramping of feet, and then the door of the laboratory flew open, and the hulking figure of Ngila stepped inside.

"Good, my friend, you have finally returned," said Doctor Steele. "Come and meet our visitor, Mr. Stone."

Ngila frowned.

"Also have visitor," he said. He then turned, stepped back into the hallway, and, moments later, reappeared with a prostrate woman lying across his huge arms.

I looked at the woman's face, and immediately recognized her.

"That's Sandra Barton!" I shouted.

Chapter Eleven
Catherine Steele

Ngila howled as the long, thin whip crackled across his back. It snapped back into the air and then came crashing down upon him once again. It slid across his back like a tongue of fire, causing him to groan in agony.

"Why did you bring the girl here?" shouted Luther. "You have given me another problem."

The whipping continued for several minutes, until finally, Ngila fell to one knee, his back bruised and bloodied. "I trust you will not break the rules next time," said Luther, the whip dangling at his side.

"Will no break rules," Ngila groaned.

"Very good. Now put on your coat, it's time to eat."

Ngila picked up his black coat and slid his arms inside. He winced as the garment fell upon his injured back.

"Here is your dinner," said Luther, standing near a table in the middle of the small white room. "Sit down and eat."

Ngila calmly approached the table and sat down on one of the chairs. He stared at the plate of food before him.

"There's a steak for you. I hope it is to your liking."

"Steak good," replied Ngila. He bent down toward the food and grabbed the steak with his hands. He then took a large bite and began to chew the juicy piece of meat.

"Yes, we have made great progress," said Luther, watching Ngila's actions. "It was only a few years ago that you had a very different reaction to the eating of meat."

"Like meat."

"I know you do. You have gone through great changes and are now no different than any other human being."

"Ngila different. Stronger."

Luther frowned. "Sometimes too much for your own good."

Ngila took another bite of the steak and began to chew.

"Is there anything wrong, Ngila?"

"Too many people on Ngila's land. Ngila need room to live."

"A common complaint of those living in the city. Why does Ngila need so much room?"

"Need room to live." He paused for a moment. "Room to mate. Time again to mate for Ngila. Make little ones."

"And why is that so important?"

"Something Ngila must do."

"Yes, yes, you hear the call of nature, continuation of the species, the purpose of life on earth. Though one wonders just what the reason is. You'd think we would have realized the folly of it all by now."

"Need to mate."

"Yes, God has decreed it."

Ngila stopped chewing and looked at Luther. "God?" he asked.

"The spiritual force that guides us all. Don't you believe in God, Ngila?"

"Yes, believe."

"A regular zealot, aren't you?"

"Believe," repeated Ngila. "Believe."

A smile inched its way across Luther's solemn face. "I wonder how the chosen would react to that statement."

Ngila looked at Luther, failing to comprehend the meaning of his remark. Then Luther turned towards me and smiled again.

"Well, my dear," he said. "What do you think of this discussion?"

"Very interesting," I replied, knowing Luther would have a hard time accepting any kind of criticism.

"Believe in God. Believe."

I heard Ngila's words and knew he was intent on mating once again. But that really didn't matter, there was a much more important issue. Although I had feared dealing with the subject, I now no longer had any choice. There was no doubt about it. Ngila was becoming a man.

I thought about all the time we had spent nurturing him. All the days we had spent teaching him English and helping him to live. I had enjoyed those days, but now began to question whether we had done the right thing. As much as I loved Ngila, I wondered whether both he and us would have been better off if Luther had never begun the experiment. We had lost most of our friends and relatives in the process, until we had become outcasts among those we had once known and loved, exiles among those we had once trusted.

It had not always been that way. When I first met Luther, we were both young and optimistic about a seemingly boundless future. Luther had just finished medical school, and I, my studies in psychology. We were young and in love, with expectations of economic freedom. But, soon, I realized Luther was more interested in research than amassing material wealth, and because I was very much in love with him, it became my interest, too.

We spurned money and embraced idealism, hoping to make discoveries that would improve human existence. "Human progress" was the phrase Luther always used. He believed in it fervently and, in time, so did I. He convinced me our research was far more important than a mundane medical practice. We, instead, would try to make a difference.

We would attempt to produce evidence that it was possible to create a more peaceful and intelligent human being who could live in harmony with the environment. To do so, we knew we would have to unlock the secrets of the human brain.

Through the years, we both steadily pursued our goal. Experimenting in genetics and the workings of the brain, Luther had obtained some successful results. Meanwhile, I worked on the psychological aspects, concentrating on behavioral abnormalities. It was then Luther joined Biocea Systems, and his work there allowed him to delve into genetic engineering and biotechnology. He began experimenting with organisms, modifying them through the artificial manipulation of their DNA. He began with bacteria, creating organisms capable of synthesizing human insulin, human growth hormone, and other medically useful substances. He attempted to correct genetic diseases by replacing defective genes with normal ones.

The microorganisms produced by recombinant DNA research began to be patented, and the government approved the sale of various genetically altered bacteria and plants. Even the Supreme Court ruled that "a live human-made microorganism is patentable matter." The ruling helped establish such commercial firms as Biocea. It also lent tacit approval to the genetic experiments of Luther and others, who used the techniques of genetic engineering, such as splicing, transplantation, and chemical replantation of repressed, nonfunctional genes.

Some of the experiments included transplanting a human gene from one species to another to produce a useable product. Patents were sought for animals that had been created through the use of human embryo cells and could be used for organ transplantation. Other experiments included creating edible birds and mammals with minimal brain functions, such as lacking consciousness, which could then be used for food without any protests about the cruelty involved. Luther was one of those involved in the many experiments. And then came Ngila.

I had relished the idea of raising this being, hoping to utilize all the techniques I had worked so hard to master. He was everything Luther and I could have hoped for. We never had found the time to have children of our own, and so, I regarded Ngila as a chance to renew our love and our lives. I resolved to teach him as our own, but as time went on, I realized Luther regarded him only as an experiment. He berated Ngila, kept him locked up for long periods of time, and regularly beat him. He explained to me that he was a simpleton, and that to treat him as our own would be foolhardy. I argued with him at first, and then, through time, quietly acquiesced. And now the years had passed, and Ngila was now fully grown.

"We will allow him to mate," Luther finally decided. "It is the only way to hopefully ameliorate his violent personality."

He glanced at me, hoping to gain my approval, hoping I still believed in the importance of the work we had dedicated our lives to. I looked back at him, still admiring his tenacity and intellect, and slowly nodded in agreement.

Chapter Twelve
Hudge Stone

I stared down at Sandra Barton, still lying unconscious in the middle of the large white room. I had attempted to awaken her without success. As I stood staring at her, I noticed how tranquil and angelic her face appeared in the midst of unfettered slumber. I studied it, the glistening smoothness of her cheeks, the subtle glint of innocence pervading her eyebrows, the gentle flow of her forehead peeking through the soft undulations of her hair. I studied the petite outline of her nose, the sensual fullness of her lips. I stood there, mesmerized, wanting to awaken her, and yet, grateful for the chance to admire her as she slept.

As I watched her, I was slowly falling in love with the slumbering creature before me. I bent down, brushed a lock of hair from her face, and kissed her on the lips. I never felt such an overwhelming desire to do such a thing in my life, even though it violated my code of ethics as a human being and a reporter. It was an act committed by the lewd and depraved, subjects of innumerable articles I had written in the past, and as I withdrew my mouth, a rush of guilt welled up inside me.

Regretting this spontaneous act of passion, I drew away from her, hoping she would not awaken. I watched her eyes, my face still inches away, and was startled by how quickly they opened. She stared at me, her face enveloped in confusion.

"Mr. Stone, what are you doing here?" she wondered.

I stammered for a moment, hoping she was unaware of my most recent action.

"We're inside the Biocea Systems building, prisoners of a Doctor Steele," I said.

"And the monster?"

"He's with Doctor Steele."

"Then we're alone?"

I nodded. "I was just trying to awaken you."

She smiled. "I enjoyed it."

I smiled back, feeling as if a weight had been lifted from my shoulders. "You understand I regret having to employ such a drastic method."

She smiled again.

I stood up, encouraged by her reply, and lifted her to her feet. "I'm sorry, Miss Barton, I didn't mean to be so bold."

"Call me Sandra, and it was better than being kissed by the monster."

"He kissed you?"

She nodded, bringing tears to her eyes. "I think he's in love with me."

"Well, I can understand that."

Sandra looked at me and smiled. It quickly faded, however, as she thought once again about the monster. "Oh, Mr. Stone, it was awful," she finally said.

I threw my arms around her and let her bury her head in my chest. "We've got to get out of here," I whispered.

She looked up at me, tears running down her cheeks. "But he'll find us. Wherever we go, he'll find us."

"That's why I have to get back to the newspaper. I have to get in touch with Doctor Quant."

"Doctor Quant?"

"He's someone who I think knows a lot about the monster. He'll probably be able to come up with some solution."

"But he's in love with me," she interrupted.

"Well, if I can get back to the newspaper, I think I can put an end to all of this."

She looked up at me, her arms still around my waist. "I don't want him to touch me again."

"Neither do I, but we may not have a choice."

"What do you mean?"

"I mean you might have to endure it if it helps us find a way to escape."

"I don't know if I can. I mean, he's so horrible."

"Listen to me, Sandra. He's not a monster. His name is Ngila and he's part of some DNA study being done by Doctor Steele. All we have to do is convince the doctor to let us go."

"But how?"

I shook my head. "I don't know, but we have to think of something."

We let go of each other, still in a daze, and walked back toward some chairs. We sat down, looked at each other, and fell silent.

"I'm sorry about Rob," I finally said.

"Poor Rob," she replied. "He didn't realize how right he was."

"About what?"

"How dangerous the park really is. Who would have believed something was running around killing people?"

"Nobody believed it."

"I know. I saw you for the first time in the park when I was trying to convince the police that a monster existed."

"I remember. I would have believed you."

"Yes, I read your stories. They were very good."

"I wonder how many people would believe us now," I said.

She looked at me and smiled, shaking her head. "Not very many. Not until they see him with their own eyes."

"I guess I can't blame them. I would feel the same way."

Sandra glanced toward the large black door, stood up, and wearing a look of apprehension, began to shout. "Let us out of here! Can anybody hear me?"

"They'll come for us eventually," I said, attempting to calm her.

"But we're going to starve to death," she replied. She then turned and ran to the door. Grabbing the doorknob, she twisted it in a desperate panic. "Let us out of here!" she shouted, hitting the door repeatedly with the palms of her hands.

She began to sob, kicking the door, and pleading with her captors. I watched the sudden display of emotion and rushed to her side. As I reached her, she turned around, and draped her arms over my shoulders.

"Don't worry, Sandra, we'll get out of here," I said, kissing her cheek. "You can count on it."

"But what are they going to do to us? I dread to even think about it."

"I won't let anything happen to you," I said, holding her tight. "Don't worry, we'll find a way out."

She stared into my eyes, looking for a certain gentle strength inside, and kissed me on the lips. I responded, and we fell into a passionate embrace. After a few moments, she struggled out of my arms and began to sob.

"What's the matter?" I asked.

"Don't fall in love with me, Hudge. I'm bad luck."

"What do you mean?"

"You don't know anything about me. Any man who falls in love with me ends up regretting it. Rob was only one of many. And now to top it all off, this monster, or whatever you want to call him, decides he's in love with me, too."

I looked at her for a second, and didn't know what to say. "And what about me? Do you think it's so easy for me to give my love? I know only murder and death. Why, it's hard to have any feelings of tenderness at all after witnessing so much hate and destruction."

"Well, aren't we two of a kind," she said, wiping her eyes. "It seems we both have had our difficulties with the rigors of romance."

We looked at each other, and I stepped toward her. Before I could reach her, the doorknob snapped, and the door opened. We could see Doctor Steele enter the room with a tray of food in one hand and a gun in the other.

"Hello, my friends, would you mind stepping back toward the table and chairs?" he said.

I grabbed Sandra's hand and we walked back across the room.

"When are you going to let us go?" asked Sandra, as she sat down in one of the chairs.

"All in good time, my friends," Doctor Steele replied. "For now, I think it's best for you to eat something."

"At least, you're not going to let us starve," said Sandra.

"Right you are, my dear. You're much too important to Ngila for me to let you die such a senseless death."

"I don't want to see that madman anymore," Sandra replied. "Don't you understand?"

"Don't talk like that, my dear. Ngila is very fond of you. He has come all the way to this country for some compassion. I don't want him to be disappointed."

"By killing people?"

"A cultural misunderstanding, I assure you, my dear. Ngila is still learning the inestimable value of human life."

"How? By keeping us prisoners?" I asked.

"It won't be very long, my friend. I first must be sure you can be trusted with the telling of Ngila's story. Now, please, my friends, eat and we will talk later."

We looked down at the metal tray before us. It contained a variety of meat and vegetables.

"Why don't you tell me more about Ngila?" I asked, inviting Doctor Steele to sit down. The doctor took a few steps forward, was about to say something, when I noticed he had lowered his gun. Grabbing the metal tray, I flung it at the doctor.

"Run, Sandra!" I shouted, leaping on top of the startled doctor.

Sandra dashed across the room as we struggled on the floor. She slipped past the open door, and hurried into the hallway. I had successfully knocked the gun from Doctor Steele's hand, preparing to attempt my own escape. I was halfway across the room when Sandra appeared once again, this time enshrouded in Ngila's arms.

"You stay," said Ngila with an angry sneer.

He then lowered Sandra to the floor, and pushed her into the room.

"What are you going to do to us?" she shouted.

"Will not hurt you," replied Ngila. "You stay."

"Yes, my friends, we suggest you stay with us for a while," interjected Doctor Steele, having regained the gun. "I'm sorry, but now you will have to go without dinner. The choice was yours."

"How long are you going to keep us here?" I angrily asked.

"Time will tell, my friend," the doctor replied. He then turned toward Ngila, motioned to him, and followed him out of the room.

I looked at Sandra, who began to sob. The sound of the door being locked echoed across the room.

It was several hours before the large black door opened once again. Sandra and I were huddled together on a gray sofa that had been left against one of the walls, when we saw Ngila's hulking body appear. We were startled at first, then calmed ourselves, as we watched him slowly make his way across the room.

Watching us, Ngila halted several feet away, looking at us curiously. "Doctor want to know if you're all right," he finally said in a low, guttural voice.

"Tell him we're hungry and tired and would very much like to leave," I said.

"No leave. You stay."

"If you insist. I guess we have no choice."

Ngila sneered, turned around, and plodded back toward the door.

"Hey, Ngila, what is this preference you have for killing people?" I shouted at him.

The hunched figure suddenly halted and slowly turned around. "Defending myself," he replied.

"But why do you have to eat them?"

"Must keep strong. People's spirits keep Ngila strong."

I looked at Sandra. "He's more primitive than I thought," I said. "Sounds like a tribesman whose beliefs are based upon superstition. It seems he has no idea the difference between right and wrong."

"Then we'd better be careful," said Sandra. "We don't want to get him too upset."

"Don't worry, I'm just going to try to reason with him. As long as we're prisoners here, we might as well attempt to get to know him. Anything he tells us will be invaluable to any articles I write. Think of it, an exclusive interview with the Monster of Central Park. Why, circulation would go through the roof."

"I think our lives are more important than selling a few newspapers," she replied. "You'd better be very careful. Our lives may depend on it."

I nodded, and then turned back toward Ngila. "Don't you think it's wrong to kill?"

Sandra winced. "What are you doing, Hudge?" she whispered. "I thought you weren't going to ask him anything that might make him violent."

Ngila looked at us and sneered. "Does not man kill?" he asked.

"Yes," I answered, "but it's wrong."

"Man wrong all the time, kill all the time. Kill to take land, kill all the animals until they no longer exist. Man kill all the time. Kill for his

God, kill for his country. Then he says killing is wrong. Wrong for others he means. Not wrong when he wants something."

"But there has to be a reason, an ideal, something worth fighting for," I said. "Man doesn't kill without a reason."

Ngila looked at me and sneered once again. "Man kills when he wants to kill. He kills the animals without reason. He kills other men without reason. I am a man. Do not tell me it is wrong to kill."

"Well, maybe human beings do kill for sport, but they don't eat their fellow human beings."

"Man kills man all the time. Makes war all the time. Kills man."

"But eating someone, that's a violation of the sanctity of life. Don't you believe in God?"

Ngila nodded. "Believe. Man believes in God, but does everything he can to hurt his fellow man. He believes in himself. I believe in me."

"Who told you all this, Ngila?" I asked.

"Doctor."

"Doctor Steele?"

Ngila looked at me and nodded. "Doctor tell Ngila many things. Teach Ngila about man and God."

"What about love, Ngila?"

"That, too." He looked at Sandra and lifted his arm. "You, mate."

Sandra turned toward me. "Now you see what you've done? You made him think about me."

"What does Ngila mean by that word?" I asked.

Ngila stared at Sandra. "Ngila love her."

Upon hearing the words, Sandra stood up and walked toward him. "You don't love me, Ngila," she said. "Can't you see that?"

"You, mate."

"But I'm not your mate," argued Sandra. "Can't you see that that's wrong?"

"No, right," growled Ngila. "You, mate." He then lunged forward and grabbed her, enveloping her in his massive arms. She screamed as he seized her, causing me to jump up and charge toward the hulking figure.

"Let her go, do you hear me?" I shouted.

I then tore at Ngila's massive body. Ngila responded with a swipe of one of his arms, sending me sprawling across the floor.

"Are you hurt?" asked Sandra anxiously, as she slipped underneath Ngila's other arm and ran toward me.

I shook my head.

Ngila watched as Sandra bent over me. She was brushing back my hair and worrying about my health.

"Is she your mate?" he finally asked.

Sandra looked at me and remained silent. The question made us both wonder about the state of our relationship. It was then the sound of the doorknob interrupted our thoughts, and Doctor Steele stepped into the room.

"Ngila!" he shouted. "What is the problem here?"

Ngila turned his head. "Defending myself," he said.

Doctor Steele glanced at me, as I was still lying on the floor. "You should have more sense than to try to overpower Ngila, Stone. Why, look at him. I'd say he has the strength of ten men. Quite beyond the limits of your paltry capabilities."

"Well, tell him to stay away from Sandra," I replied.

"Oh, so Miss Barton was the cause of this misunderstanding. Ngila seems to think of you as his mate."

Sandra stood up and glared at Doctor Steele. "Yes, and I wish you would explain to him the error he has made. I don't know how they treat women wherever he came from, but he has a lot to learn about being a gentleman."

"I very much agree, Miss Barton, which is why I had you brought here. You see I'm counting on you to help change him, make him more of a man."

"Not me," she replied. "I'm sorry, doctor, but you have the wrong girl."

"We'll see about that," said Doctor Steele. "In the meantime, I'll give you some time to think it over."

He then turned toward Ngila.

"Come," he said, "there is much work to be done."

Ngila grunted, looked back at Sandra, and followed Doctor Steele out of the room.

Chapter Thirteen
An Eyewitness Report

I saw a man walking home beneath the streetlights, approaching his apartment building, when I heard something grunting in the distance. It sounded like an animal, and when the man whirled around, he was met by the vicious stare of some hulking, monstrous creature.

He was going to scream, but instead, seemed fascinated by the enormity of the huge figure. When the creature lurched forward, however, he dropped his briefcase and began running down the sidewalk. He was about to reach the door of his apartment building, when the creature suddenly grabbed him and tossed him onto the pavement. He fell hard, looked up, and could see the creature holding a long, white bone in his hand. Then I heard a loud grunt, and the bone came crashing down upon his head. There was blood oozing across his forehead, but it appeared he was too old to do anything about it. The creature kept pounding him with the bone.

I watched as the creature kept striking the man's head until he had smashed his skull. He then reached down and began pulling the skull apart. Brains began oozing out of the shattered skull, blood running down the side of the man's face. The creature began tearing away at the exposed brain, eagerly eating what seeped out through the skull. When the skull had finally been pulled completely apart, the creature sank his teeth into the half-eaten brain.

The creature then celebrated his triumph with contented grunts. After the brain had been devoured, he pulled the man to the side of the road and began walking back toward the river.

ANOTHER EYEWITNESS REPORT BY NEIGHBOR, LINDA BARTLETT

A crowd of people had gathered around Bernie Krantz's blood-soaked body. His wife, Ruth, stood nearby screaming in the night, alternately shouting and sobbing about the horrifying incident that had taken place. When she saw the police finally arrive, she began running toward them.

"Oh, thank God," she wailed. "Please help me, someone's killed my Bernie. Oh, it's horrible, horrible."

The officers emerged from their car, and glanced at the body. They stared at the shattered skull and the bloodied face frozen in shock and terror.

"You have any idea who might have done this?" one of them asked Ruth.

"Bernie didn't have an enemy in the world," she replied. "Oh, my poor Bernie. It's horrible, simply horrible."

"Well, it looks like the work of that so-called monster. Did anybody see anything?"

Someone in the crowd, a man with a gray beard and graying hair, stepped forward.

"Why, his brain is completely gone," someone murmured, pointing at the body.

Chapter Fourteen
Hudge Stone

"We've got to escape," said Sandra, nervously tapping her hand on the table. She glanced at me. I was lying on the gray sofa.

"I don't see how," I replied. "There are no windows in the room, the door is securely locked, and even if we manage to get out of here, there's Ngila to deal with."

"But we must," she replied, slapping her hand down on the table. "Don't you understand? That monster is in love with me. Who knows what he wants from me? I can't bear to think about it. We just have to get out of here."

"We already tried. I mean, he threw me away like I was a toy. The only chance we have is getting Doctor Steele alone. But I don't see how that will happen. Ngila follows him around everywhere he goes."

"Isn't there some way to open that door? We can sneak out in the middle of the night. They wouldn't know we were gone until morning."

"That's a pretty solid lock on that door. I've already tried, but I have no tools, and there's nothing in here we can use. I'm afraid we're just going to have to wait."

"Wait?" she shouted. "Wait until I get raped by that monster? Wait until he decides to eat one of us? Wait until when, Hudge?"

"I don't know," I replied. "I just don't see any way to escape. Don't you think I want to get out of here just as much as you do? I mean, you may become his bride, but me, I'm just another meal to him. And what happens when Doctor Steele decides he no longer has any use for me?"

"Well, we just can't sit around and wait for the worst to happen. There's got to be something we can do."

I sat up, slowing getting to my feet. "Maybe I'll take a look at that lock again. There's got to be some way to jimmy it open. I just wish I had the proper tools."

"We'll find something," she said. "As long as we, at least, give it a try."

"What about Ngila?"

"First, let's try to get out of here, then we'll worry about him. I think maybe I can distract him long enough for us to escape. The hard part is opening this door."

I walked across the room, studied the door for a moment, and sighed. I grabbed the doorknob and gave it several violent turns. I then reached down and slipped off my shoe. Holding it firmly in my hand, I began hitting the top of the knob with the heel. After several sharp blows, I stopped.

"It's not heavy enough," I said. "See if you can find some sort of metal object. We need something heavy enough to break off this knob."

Sandra nodded and began searching the room.

"Something long and thin might work as well, although there's not much of an opening. I can't even see the lock."

I continued to examine the door as Sandra kept searching. "Find anything?" I finally shouted across the room.

"There's nothing here," she replied. "The room is completely empty except for these chairs, the table, and the sofa."

"That's what I figured," I said. "I knew they wouldn't be stupid enough to leave anything lying around. We're just going to have to wait. There's nothing else we can do. Maybe I'll rush Doctor Steele again when he brings us breakfast. Then you can distract Ngila, and maybe we'll escape. That's the best we can hope for right now."

"There's nothing else we can do?"

"Not unless you have a drill or a hammer or something like that. I mean, this door is pretty thick and it's also locked solid."

"Can't you use one of these chairs? They seem heavy enough."

I walked across the room, examined the chairs, and sighed. "I guess I'll give it a try," I finally said. "Although it's going to be pretty noisy."

She watched as I carried one of the chairs back to the door. Then picking it up over my shoulder, I flung it at the metal knob. There was a terrific crash that echoed for several moments through the room. The chair rattled to a rest, and I stepped forward to see what damage it had done.

"Just a small dent," I said. "I think I'd have to throw this chair a few hundred times to get that knob to budge. Not to mention, all the noise it's going to make."

"I think you've already alerted the entire building to our planned escape. Maybe you're right. We should wait until morning. I just wonder what he has planned for us tomorrow."

I looked at her. "Hopefully, nothing too strenuous. I only hope Ngila eats tonight — whomever it may be, poor soul. Maybe I can reason with Doctor Steele in the morning. If that doesn't work, we'll have to use force." I tried to be convincing, but a sudden yawn interrupted the solemn threat. "But first, I need some sleep," I said. "Whatever may happen, I need to get some rest."

"It has been a long day," she said with a yawn. "I wonder what time it is, anyway. Feels like it's the middle of the night."

"It might just be. Too bad he took our watches before putting us in here. Hand me one of those sofa cushions, I guess I'll sleep on the floor."

She walked over to me and kissed me on the cheek. I looked at her, yawned once again, and then knelt down upon the cushion. I placed my head on one end, and then stretched my body until my feet rested upon the floor. Sandra, meanwhile, curled up on the other cushion, her feet touching the base of the sofa.

"Good night, Sandie, my love," I mumbled, closing my eyes. "Don't worry, everything's going to work out just fine."

I thought I heard her answer, her soft words drifting through my resting mind. They gently wafted through my brain and then vanished into tranquil sleep.

In the midst of my sleep, I suddenly heard a gentle voice whispering inside my head. "Get up!" the voice said. "Please, sir, get up!"

I opened my eyes and squinted at the anxious figure before me. It was a woman wearing a white hospital gown, her stomach somewhat bloated as if she were at the beginning of a long pregnancy.

"Who are you?" I asked.

"That isn't important right now," she replied. "You've got to get up so we can get out of here."

I sat up and glanced at the keys dangling from the woman's hand. "You've come to help us escape?" I asked.

The woman nodded, than reached over and began poking Sandra, who was still asleep. "Please, we must hurry," she said. "We don't have much time."

Sandra stood up, yawned, and began slipping on her shoes.

"Follow me," the woman said. "But we must hurry."

"What's your name?"

"Molly. Molly Rogers. I was abducted by the monster and brought here. Just like you. Hurry, before they realize I'm gone."

"Are you part of some kind of experiment?" asked Sandra.

Molly looked back at her forlornly. "I'm carrying the monster's baby," she whispered. "I had no choice. It was either that or my life."

Sandra winced. "I'm so sorry, Molly," she said. "Let's get out of here. We're right behind you."

We followed her across the room and past the large black door. Stepping into a darkened hallway, we carefully made our way down the corridor.

"There's a door at the end of the hallway," said Molly. "And then we're outside."

We hurried down the corridor until Molly grabbed her stomach and slowed her pace.

"I don't feel so good," she said. "But we've got to get past that door before it's too late."

I halted, went back and took her hand, and helped her toward the door. In a few moments, we were standing in front of another big black door.

"Push it open!" Molly said. "Hurry, before they find us."

I let go of Molly's hand and approached the door. I pushed at it, but the door didn't open.

"Again!" Molly said. "Try again!"

This time, Sandra stepped next to me. She placed her hands on the door, and we then tried pushing it open together.

"It's no use," I grunted. "It won't budge."

"Try again," Molly replied. "Try using your shoulder."

I nodded and stepped away from the door. Lowering my shoulder, I took a few steps and lunged toward the door. With a screech, the door flew open, the impact sending Sandra and me sprawling to the ground. We had landed outside the building, although the door had closed behind us.

"We've got to get Molly," I said, getting to my feet. I examined the door and noticed it hadn't fully closed. Grabbing the edge, I slowly pulled it open.

"Run!" Molly shouted from inside. I peered into the darkness and could see Molly enveloped by Ngila's huge arms. I stepped back and slammed the big black door. I then grabbed Sandra's hand, and we ran down a nearby pathway toward the brightly lit avenue.

"What about Molly?" asked Sandra.

"We'll have to come back for her," I replied, pulling her across the open street. "There's no time. First, we have to escape ourselves." I glanced over my shoulder and could see Ngila peering from the corner of the building.

"Look! Ngila is right behind us!"

We continued to run until we spotted a yellow taxi slowly cruising down the avenue. We halted, waving our arms frantically in the air. The vehicle pulled up alongside us and we hurried inside.

"The *Herald* and step on it," I said, sliding into the back seat next to Sandra.

The motor roared, and the taxi sped off into the distance.

Chapter Fifteen
Ngila

Let man and woman go. Still have mate behind locked door. I ran into the shadows, between buildings. I got to open land. Park, the doctor calls it, and hid among the trees and bushes. I looked up at moon, the glowing round rock in the sky, and went back into the shadows. No one can see me, but I can see them. Silence filled the air. Ngila likes silence. I can hear the sound of a car passing along the nearby road. I don't want to be with humans, they only cause problems for me. Though I am a man, they treat me as if I am different. I go deeper into the darkness like the creatures of the jungle that disappear into the night.

After a while, I began to get tired, and sat down beneath a large tree. I closed my eyes, and soon I was gazing down at the gleaming silver stream flowing through the tangled jungle, its cool waters bubbling past the high grass. It was something I seem to remember, and yet, am not sure if I have ever been there. As I was thinking about the jungle, there was a sudden noise, the sound of footsteps among the nearby leaves and twigs. My eyes jumped open, although I didn't see anybody there. The dream had been soothing, and I stretched my arms and yawned. When I opened my eyes again, a dark form stood before me.

"Who are you?" asked a voice in the darkness.

"I am a man," Ngila replied.

"Yes, yes, and so you are."

I watched as the figure moved toward me. I could barely see an old man in dirty clothing, bent and tired. The old man leaned forward, pulling at his beard, and then began to speak.

"The park is my home, you understand," he said. "Been here for the last few years, though no fault of my own, I can tell you that."

Ngila stared at the old man, interested in his words, and remained sitting on the ground listening to him speak.

"Not like it used to be," the old man said. "More and more people all the time. You can't hardly move anymore without running into somebody. Yep, more and more people all the time. Hey, I hope you don't mind me asking, but do you happen to have any money with you?"

Ngila looked at him, not knowing what he meant. "Money?"

The old man waited for a few moments, and then looked sad, slowly putting down his arm. "Well, there's no harm in asking," he said. "I happen not to have any money myself, you understand. Nope, times sure are hard, I can tell you that. Why, used to be folks had no problem handing out a buck here and there. A man could actually survive if he had a mind to. But these days, why, everybody's out for themselves, not caring about anybody else. They just as soon as see you starve to death than to part with any of their precious possessions. You know what I mean?"

Ngila looked at him and nodded head.

"You sure are a quiet one, I can tell you that," the old man said, his fingers still pulling the clump of gray hair growing on his chin. "By looking at me, you wouldn't know I was once rich. Yep, as rich as those people on Park Avenue. Even more money than that. Well, now, I was once married, a beautiful woman she was, and I was making a pretty good living, you understand. Then the next thing I know, my wife tells me she's leaving me. Irreconcilable differences, she says. Hell, if I knew how she felt, I would've been home more often. Problem is the only thing we ever did was argue. Yep, we had some pretty good fights, I can tell you that.

"Well, anyway, after she leaves, I kind of felt like there was no purpose anymore. I mean, I didn't know why I was working so hard. Didn't make sense, didn't seem like anything about life made sense anymore. Well, that's when I started drinking. The divorce made me drink even more. Money, I had no use for it anymore. Then the wife took most of it, and I decided I would try to get some back gambling. Well, let me tell you, once you start, you can't stop, and that's a fact. Between the gambling and the drinking, I was suddenly flat broke. Lost my apartment, my wife, and all my money. But, you know, I really didn't care anymore. I realized there was no sense to any of it, just things to take our minds off how senseless life is. That's all. Anyway, I was free, you understand. So I came to the park. Have been here ever since."

"Free," Ngila said with a smile.

"That's right, freedom. Say, you haven't committed any crime or anything, have you? Not that it's any of my business, you understand. No, I guess it doesn't really matter if you have, come to think of it. I guess I'm just worried about getting mugged myself. But people usually leave you alone if you don't have anything of value to take, and that's a fact. I've been robbed before, you know. Some punk had a knife and he was threatening to cut me. Well, I gave him three dollars and he left me alone. I wasn't willing to die for that kind of money. You know what I mean?

"Anyway, you see crimes taking place around here all the time, people getting robbed or assaulted or worse. Some guy was killed in the park for no reason at all. Found his body half-eaten. Yep, that's what I heard. Some kind of monster, they say. If you ask me, there's a lot more monsters in this city than they think. I see them all the time, growling and grumbling and caring only about themselves. You know what I mean?"

Yes, Ngila know what he means. "Monsters."

"Why some little monster threw me off my bench in the middle of the night," he said, lifting a bent finger and pointing into the darkness. "No reason for it at all. Just decided I was in his territory or something. He said he was going to stab me if I didn't find some place else to sleep. Now that was a monster, I can tell you that."

The old man was silent, and then began to stare at Ngila. "Say, what are you doing in the park, anyway? You're not thinking of robbing me, are you? Because I don't have any money with me, you understand. If it's my territory you're thinking of taking, I'm quite willing to share it with you, if you don't mind. You're not hiding from the police, are you? Because if you are, that's fine by me. I have no love for them, anyway."

"No break rules," said Ngila. Old man was making Ngila upset.

Decided I would leave and look at other parts of the park. Ngila stood up, and saw the old man watching me. He was looking at Ngila's long, black coat. Then the old man began to shake like he was getting scared.

"Hey, you're not that monster fella, are you?" he asked, grabbing once again at his clump of gray hair.

"No monster," replied Ngila.

"Well, even if you are, I guess that's no business of mine. Every man is free to do whatever he likes, as far as I'm concerned. Now, where are you hurrying off to? We're just starting to get to know each other. Sit down, my friend, there's no need to go so soon. Don't mind my questions, I don't mean anything by it. Why don't you sit down and make yourself comfortable? There's no need for you to go."

Ngila listened to the old man, grunted, and sat back down on the ground.

"Now you stay there," the old man said. "I'll be back in a second. I'll get us some wine from my sack. You'll see, we'll talk and get to know each other."

Ngila watched as the old man went into the darkness. I looked at the buildings and brightly lit roads that surrounded the park. Ngila then stared at the glowing lights in the distance.

Chapter Sixteen
Hudge Stone

The taxi pulled up alongside the curb and came to a halt. Sandra and I stepped out and hurried inside the *Herald* building. When we entered the newsroom, I noticed a man with gray hair wearing a black jacket sitting near my desk, and hesitated for a moment.

"Hudge," my city editor shouted from across the room. "Knew you'd be back eventually. There's been another murder."

I looked at him and pointed at the man. "That's Doctor Quant," my editor replied. "He's been waiting for you all night. He has a very interesting story to tell you."

"Doctor Quant? Boy, am I glad to see you." I hurried across the room, holding onto Sandra's hand. When I reached Doctor Quant, he shook my hand, and I expressed my gratitude for making the trip from Washington.

"I'm glad to see you're all right, Mr. Stone," said Doctor Quant with the hint of a foreign accent. "When I heard about Doctor Lido, I hurried here as fast as I could. He had told me about speaking with you. I was afraid your life might be in danger."

"Well, we just came from a meeting with your friend, Doctor Steele. Seems he takes quite an interest in anyone asking about the National Genome Project."

"I imagine so," replied Doctor Quant. "You see, he and I are among the only ones who know the exact location of Site Seven."

I looked at him. "Site Seven?"

"Sit down, my friends, I have a lot to tell you about the genome project." Doctor Quant fell silent for a moment. "Where shall I begin? They are killers, you know. Absolute killers."

"Who are killers, doctor?" I asked, somewhat bewildered.

"Oh, yes, you did not have enough time to read the entire report — the government project to investigate the origins of man. Project Dawning. I believe Doctor Lido was hesitant about telling you what had occurred for fear that you would think it too astonishing, too implausible. But now that you have seen the creature for yourself and have talked to Doctor Steele, I think you are prepared."

"So you do know a lot about the monster, don't you, Doctor Quant?"

"Yes, my friend. I was one of those to accompany Doctor Steele to the Congo."

"The Congo?"

"That's correct. You see, as part of the genome project, we had hoped to study human evolution and migration utilizing mitochondrial DNA and the Y chromosomes to trace the history of humanity through both the female and male lines."

"What does that have to do with the Congo?"

"We decided the study would include utilizing the lowland gorillas of the area. You realize there are only about 94,000 still alive in the world. Well, anyway, these creatures, which have been subjected to extensive hunting, deforestation, and other human activities, were chosen to be studied using our knowledge of DNA. After all, according to British biologist T.H. Huxley, the structural differences that separate man from the gorilla and chimpanzee are not as great as those which separate the gorilla from the lower apes or monkeys.

"We realized many scientists still doubted whether man was a direct descendant of the present-day apes, although most agreed they shared common ancestors. Preliminary comparative studies of genetic material repeatedly demonstrated the close proximity of the African ape and modern man. Indeed, all findings agreed that apes and human beings had had a common origin within the African continent. According to Frans de Waal, the differences between "Lucy," the famed 3.2 million-year-old australopithecine fossil and present-day apes are minimal. He concluded the most significant difference between the two was in their hips, not their craniums. In fact, he wrote that the sensory systems of both were essentially the same as in humans. Our study would help prove whether this was true or not."

"But how did Doctor Steele ever get involved?" I asked.

"You see, there was a great competition, Mr. Stone, between the government and many private companies to complete the human genome project. Many of these companies, Doctor Steele's included, hoped to be the first to perform each possible study."

"He tried to kill us," I said. "And I think he's responsible for Doctor Lido's death as well."

"Yes, he'll do anything to be the first to complete the study. There's a great deal of money at stake, and Steele is determined not to let anyone or anything get in his way. Like keeping the findings at Site Seven a secret."

"What exactly is Site Seven, doctor?"

"Site Seven, Mr. Stone, was the designated area where the experiments would take place. It was located in a grassy savanna area adjacent to the Congo rain forest. We had laboratories and housing built on the site, and then we went about studying the apes."

I watched the doctor with interest. His eyes, dark brown, were filled with solemnity and insight. Every so often, he paused to quickly survey the room as if he were still worried someone violent and nefarious was listening.

"What happened?" I finally asked.

"Do you know anything about genetic engineering and biotechnology, Mr. Stone? Well, let's just say it is possible to manipulate, modify, and recombine DNA to change an organism."

"You did this to the apes?"

"Yes, we did," replied Doctor Quant. "And we soon reached a point in which their cranial capacity had almost doubled and they were almost on the verge of bipedalism. A very great evolutionary leap, indeed. Well, as you can imagine, we were extremely concerned the government would decide to terminate our funding and put an end to the experiments fearing protests from animal rights groups."

Doctor Quant hesitated for a moment.

"You must understand, there were a number of things we planned on learning from these creatures — everything from genetics to evolutionary theory, to human psychology and sociology. Why, those creatures could help unlock the secrets of the human brain." He looked down for a moment and then continued speaking. "That is why it was so important to continue the experiments.

"We called it phase two of Project Dawning. The theory was simple enough. We would utilize all the techniques of genetic engineering and biotechnology, and hopefully, produce a creature with new anatomical information that would lead to continued structural change. As you know, we had already completed mapping out the 25,000 or so genes that constitute the human being. It was, therefore, not really that difficult to change a few chromosomes and thus, change the organism."

"But what about the ethical issues involved?" I asked, keeping track of the doctor's explanation in my notebook.

"Well, the government determined it was very unethical," he replied with a sigh. "Which is exactly why I decided to leave the project a few months later. We had taken it upon ourselves to begin altering Nature, and I began to agree with the government that the experiments were not only an invasion of the sanctity of life, but downright cruel as well. I therefore returned to Washington, thereby ending the government study. Doctor Steele, however, was vehement in his defense of the program, and insisted on continuing the experiments at a site financed by Biocea."

"But you said they were killers," I said.

"They became killers, Mr. Stone," the doctor replied. "That was one of our major problems. Apparently, the anthropologists are correct. Our ancestors were probably meat-eating cannibals. Although we think of them as tree-climbing plant eaters, they also caught and ate small animals — even before the invention of stone tools. Why, according to a study of Neanderthal bones, it was found that that hominid's diet consisted of ninety percent meat. Although the DNA of Neanderthal seems to be somewhat different than modern man, they were no doubt similar to man in that they were both excellent hunters.

"As far as killing each other, one only has to refer to Hobbes, who said, in his natural state, man is in a continual state of war. Raymond Dart was among those anthropologists who suggested this included cannibalism. Indeed, the most recent studies have shown that Neanderthals, who lived about 300,000 years ago, did, in fact, kill and eat their own kind. The objective was to eat enough fat along with their meat to help them survive the harsh European winter. Brains, as well as bone marrow, are very high in fat, you see. Other scientists suggest they may have eaten their enemies or practiced cannibalism after a natural death. The reasons are still open to debate, although the fact that they engaged in cannibalism has already been proven beyond a reasonable doubt."

"Sounds very much like Ngila," I said.

"Yes," agreed Sandra. "It sounds very much like the monster."

"Do you realize the word, *ngila*, is from the Mbeti dialect," said Doctor Quant. "It means, gorilla."

"Then you think Ngila was one of those gorillas he experimented on in the Congo?"

"I don't really know. I would be very curious to examine the composition of that creature's DNA."

"But what if Ngila really is an ape?" I asked. "Isn't he then more dangerous than we thought?"

"If he was originally an ape, he's not an ordinary gorilla, I can tell you that," replied Doctor Quant. "I mean, with the methods of genetic engineering and biotechnology anything is really possible."

"Well, we just have to put an end to it, that's all," I said. "We can't allow this creature to run around killing people. He's invoking evolutionary rules that no longer apply to the human race."

"Maybe not," said Doctor Quant, staring strangely at his listeners. "Remember, my friends, we, too, are being hunted. Whether you realize it or not, these experiments are very valuable to Biocea and the results could be worth millions of dollars. Our only hope is to inform the people of what is going on. You see, the public tends to frown upon scientists playing God, especially when it's in the name of the almighty dollar. Once the people learn of the experiments, I'm quite sure there will be endless accusations of cruelty and irresponsibility. I believe there's nothing that Biocea won't do to try to stop us from telling the world."

"Well, we'll just have to be careful," I replied. "It's our duty to tell the American people what Biocea is doing. It's one of the requirements of a free society and press."

Sandra looked at me admiringly and softly touched my hand. "Are you going to write a story about all this, Hudge?" she asked.

"Although I probably should, I think I'd like to speak with Doctor Steele one more time. Besides, we have to do something to rescue Molly. She's still trapped inside that damned building."

"What do you propose, my friend?" asked Doctor Quant.

"I think we should pay our friend, Doctor Steele, a visit. We'll confront him with the information we have, and then see what he says about Ngila. Whether we put an end to it or not, I'll have the copy I need to expose the Project Dawning study once and for all."

Sandra wrapped her hand around mine and stared into my eyes. "Don't you think it's too dangerous, Hudge?" she asked.

"Maybe," I replied. "But it's the only way. I need more information about Ngila before I publish anything. And only Doctor Steele can supply that information. Hopefully, we can persuade him to release Molly and tell us everything he knows about the experiment. Once I publish the information, Biocea will probably no longer wish to harm us because the study will be a matter of public record."

"When do we go, my friend?" asked Doctor Quant.

I thought for a moment, then glanced at Sandra. "I think we should wait until daylight. If we're not out of there by the time the sun goes down, Sandra can call the police and let them know where we are. In the meantime, I'm going to leave my notes here at the paper in case anything does happen to us. That way, nothing will prevent some story from appearing in the paper."

"Oh, Hudge, I hope you know what you're doing," said Sandra. "You may end up in that room again, and this time, without any chance of escaping. I hope this story is important enough to risk your life."

"There's no other way. Somebody has to find out the truth and put an end to all of this."

"I'm afraid I must agree with Mr. Stone," said Doctor Quant. "No one knows Doctor Steele's ultimate plans. We must stop him before he carries them out."

"All of this, I gather, will be done in the interests of science and money," I said. "I fail to see how any scientist can justify all the destruction, no matter how much money is at stake. That's the problem with science, all the bodies they leave behind."

"But think of the knowledge we eventually gain, my friend," replied Doctor Quant.

"At what price?" I asked. "At what price?"

Chapter Seventeen
Ngila

"Drink up!" laughed the old man. He pulled at the piece of gray hair hanging from his chin. He watched as I held the bottle of wine over my head and drank. The purple liquid spilled from Ngila's lips and down on my black coat.

"Yes, my friend, nothing like it in the world, I can tell you that," said the old man. "It will take all the harshness of living away, and that's a fact."

Ngila kept drinking until bottle was empty. He gave it back to the old man. Ngila swung his arm over his face and wiped his lips and chin with the sleeve of his coat. Ngila wanted more.

"Good," Ngila grunted.

"That's true, sure enough," said the old man. "Best stuff in the world, I can tell you that. And now, my friend, why don't you tell me something about yourself?"

"A man," I replied. "I am a man."

"Nothing much to being a man, that's for sure. Where do you come from, anyway?"

"Far away."

"Well, I could've guessed that. From across the water, I imagine."

Ngila nodded. "From jungle."

"Is that a fact? I'm from a jungle, too." The old man fell silent. "New York City," he finally said with a laugh.

Ngila looked at him and frowned. "Not jungle," I replied with a shake of my head.

"All depends on how you look at it," said the old man. "Why, some of the people here are more ferocious than any tiger. They'd eat you up in a second without thinking twice. Yep, man-eaters, the lot of them. Only it's not flesh they feed upon, it's your very soul."

"Soul?"

"Why, your living spirit. The essence of your material existence. Why, your soul, man!"

"Do not know about soul," Ngila said, beginning to feel dizzy from the wine. "But need people's spirits to keep Ngila strong."

"What's that you say?" asked the old man. "You need people's spirits?"

"Spirits keep Ngila strong."

"And how do you obtain those spirits, my friend?"

"Eat them."

"What's that? You mean you invite them over for dinner? Well, I should like to attend one of your soirees, if you don't mind. Sounds like it would be a perfectly enjoyable event."

"Ngila eat *them*."

The old man was silent again and looked at me. "You don't mean to say? Now, I hope that's not the wine talking. Eat them, huh? Why, that's perfectly savage." He tilted the wine bottle and drank what was left. "On the other hand, I imagine it's a fine cure for overpopulation. Eat or be eaten, is that it, my friend? Well, I can safely say most of them have it coming to them, anyway." The old man laughed once again. "And how do we taste? Ghastly, I'm sure."

I was surprised at what the old man said. "People good," I said.

"And how many have you eaten?" asked the old man.

"Many," replied Ngila. "Doctor let me hunt at night."

"A doctor oversees these proceedings?"

Ngila nodded.

"Strangest therapy I ever heard of, I can tell you that. Now let me see. What we need is another bottle of wine. Yes, that's it. Now you stay here, my friend, and relax. I will go and get us some more wine. We have much more to talk about."

"Wine good," said Ngila. "Will stay."

The old man nodded his head. He stood up, went into the darkness. Ngila watched him and grunted his approval. When the old man didn't return after a few moments, Ngila placed his head down and closed his eyes. He was feeling quite sleepy and longed to dream once again of the shining silver stream. Then, as if by magic, I closed my eyes and fell away into darkness. I was once again standing in the middle of the green jungle. I looked around, but could see only the bubbling stream.

Then I saw an ape standing by the stream. I watched as the ape bent down and began to drink, and then Ngila stepped forward into the light.

"I am a man," I said to the ape.

The ape looked at me, growled, and then hurried off into the bushes.

"I am a man," I said.

The apes then returned, and began throwing stones at me again. Ngila snarled at them, but the stones kept flying through the air. "I am a man," Ngila shouted.

Then I opened my eyes and looked for the old man. He suddenly appeared with another man in blue, a policeman.

Ngila ran into the darkness. There was the sound of an explosion, and Ngila felt the pain once again. Ngila's arm was burning, but kept running into the bushes. There was blood on me, and I knew I must find doctor. Doctor will help Ngila. Doctor is Ngila's friend.

Chapter Eighteen
Hudge Stone

The sun glistened amid a deep blue sky as the taxi pulled up to the curb. Sandra, Doctor Quant, and I stepped out and stood staring at the building squatting in the distance.

"That's it," I said. "Are you sure you want to go inside with me, doctor?"

"Nothing would please me more, Mr. Stone. You forget, Doctor Steele and I are old friends. I imagine we'll have much to talk about."

"I'm glad you feel that way because I was having some doubts myself about going back inside."

"There's nothing to worry about," said Doctor Quant. "I doubt if Doctor Steele will do anything to harm us. I'm sure he realizes the secret of the Project Dawning study would eventually be exposed."

"Don't be so sure," interjected Sandra. "He seemed very protective of his experiment. He probably has already killed and will kill again to keep it a secret. And who knows who or what that Ngila really is."

"All the more reason for this undertaking," replied Doctor Quant. "I should like to examine Ngila very much. I believe the results could be quite fascinating."

"Well, I'm not going back in there again," said Sandra. "I've had just about enough of that Ngila for an entire lifetime. You forget, he's in love with me."

"As you wish, my dear," replied Doctor Quant. "It is well that one of us should stand outside in case anything happens. I'm sure the police would be very pleased to know the location of the monster they are so ardently hunting for. All I ask is that you give us an adequate amount of time before you decide to supply that revelation. It would be a shame not to be able to make a full and complete determination. Would you not agree, Mr. Stone?"

"Completely, doctor. Once the police are involved, I doubt if we would have the chance to obtain the answers we both are looking for. As for me, this story could be the pinnacle of my career. It is the stuff of Pulitzers and worldwide exclusives."

Sandra looked at me. "Is it more important than me, Hudge?"

"Of course not."

"Well, I would like to see you come out of there alive," she said.

I stopped walking and gazed into her eyes. I had fallen in love with this woman, and apparently, she had done the same. Amid all the commotion, I hadn't really thought about it until that very moment.

"Don't worry, Sandie," I finally said. "I'll come back. It's just this story means so much to both of us."

"What do you mean?"

"It's a chance for us to have a good life together, don't you see? If I can get an exclusive out of all this, why we might be able to actually settle down. It just might give us the chance to dream."

I walked over to her and gently kissed her on the lips. "It's that important?" she asked.

I slowly nodded my head.

"Well, in that case, I'll wait as long as I can, but not a second more."

I smiled and put my arm around her. "That's what I was hoping you would say."

I kissed her again, then stepped back, and hurried toward Doctor Quant, who was waiting a few feet away. "Remember," I said, looking back at Sandra, "wait as long as you can."

Sandra nodded her head and waved. I waved back, following Doctor Quant toward the building.

"Now how shall we get in?" the doctor asked.

"Through the back door. That way, we'll be able to surprise him and, hopefully, convince him to give us the answers we need."

I led Doctor Quant down the narrow pathway that ran alongside the building, and halted in front of a big black door. Grabbing the handle, I attempted to pull it open. I struggled with it for a few moments, then wondering whether it was locked, stepped back toward Doctor Quant.

"I'm not really sure if it's stuck or locked," I said. "It's the same door we used to escape. I had hoped I would be able to get it open."

"Don't worry, Mr. Stone. If we have to use the front entrance, so be it. As long as we get to talk to Doctor Steele."

"But that's just the problem. Will we get to see Doctor Steele? He may try to avoid us if we give him the chance."

It was then we heard the sound of groaning drifting from one of the nearby alleyways.

"I think someone's coming," I whispered. "Let's hide behind the building."

We hurried around the corner of the building, and then sufficiently hidden, peered out into the sunlight. We could still hear the groaning, and realized whoever it was, was in great pain. The sound got closer, until a hulking figure in a black coat stumbled out of the alleyway and into the light. Doctor Quant gasped at the sight of him.

We watched as Ngila stepped toward the black door, and with one mighty tug, pulled the door open and stepped inside. Seeing that the door remained open, I leaped into the sunlight and grabbed it before it closed. I motioned to Doctor Quant and we followed Ngila inside.

The hallway was dimly lit, and when the door was closed, the darkness enveloped us. We huddled in one corner and watched as Ngila slowly plodded down the corridor. When he reached one of the doors, he knocked, and after a moment, out stepped Doctor Steele.

"Ngila, what has happened?" we could hear him say in a concerned voice. Then there was a shuffling of feet and they disappeared down an adjoining hallway.

Hearing the footsteps fading in the distance, Doctor Quant and I emerged from the shadows. We walked slowly down the hallway until I spotted another black door and halted.

"This is the room where Sandra and I were held hostage," I said, pointing at the door. "I'm sure they'll come back here sooner or later."

I approached the door and twisted the handle. The door opened, and we stepped inside.

"Looks like this was a laboratory at one time," said Doctor Quant, noticing the black laboratory table near one of the walls.

"I think it's used as some sort of guest room now," I replied, walking toward the gray sofa, chairs, and white table. "Although I don't think you'd want to be one of their guests."

"I don't plan on staying, Mr. Stone, although I would like to examine that creature. An extraordinary specimen, if I do say so. He must be a product of the Project Dawning experiments."

"No one would know better than you, doctor."

"I can't be sure, you understand, but I would say that creature is not human. Although to be perfectly honest, I am thoroughly amazed."

"Well, I think our friend, Doctor Steele, will be able to explain everything eventually."

"But to see that creature standing there…Why, he must be a result of the experiments."

"Well, we'll find out soon enough, doctor. I wonder what happened to him, anyway. It looked as if he was bleeding."

"That doesn't surprise me. As long as he is walking around, anything is bound to happen. I only wonder how many people he's been responsible for killing already. It's Doctor Steele who's to blame for all of this. I should think there has been quite a lot of blood spilled over this whole affair due to Doctor Steele's stubborn insistence to keep the

Project Dawning study a secret."

We waited for what seemed like hours, alternately discussing Ngila, Doctor Steele, and the details of the Project Dawning study. We intently watched the big black door, and not seeing anyone enter, finally decided to search for Doctor Steele. Quietly opening the door, we stepped out into the hallway. We kept walking until we reached another intersecting corridor.

"I think I hear Doctor Steele's voice," I whispered. "He must be in one of these rooms."

"Very good, Mr. Stone," replied Doctor Quant. "I am quite content to follow you."

Walking down the corridor, we noticed an open door to our right. We carefully stepped toward it, our bodies up against the hallway wall. When we finally reached the opening, we could hear the unmistakable sound of Doctor Steele's voice.

I motioned to Doctor Quant, and we peered inside. There on an operating table sat Ngila, softly grunting, while Doctor Steele attended to his injured arm.

"That should be better for now, my friend," said Doctor Steele. "But I suggest you be more careful next time. Are you sure the police didn't follow you?"

Ngila nodded.

I looked at Doctor Quant, hoping for a signal of some kind, when the doctor suddenly stepped forward and entered the room.

"Oh, they'll be here soon enough, doctor," he said.

Doctor Steele turned quickly, and then without a sound, gazed at Doctor Quant as if he had been expecting him. Ngila also turned, but his reaction was quite different. He began to snarl.

"It's quite all right, Ngila," said Doctor Steele. "Quant here is an old friend. It has been a long time, doctor."

"It appears the streets of New York City are more dangerous than the jungles of the Congo."

"Indeed. Ngila here has been shot."

"It's not unexpected. The study never was meant to be conducted in the midst of a busy modern city."

"An oversight, I'm sure, for you see the city has been quite helpful to Ngila's development as an intelligent human being."

"Are you sure, Steele? From what I've heard, Ngila is nothing more than a fearsome killer."

Ngila sneered at the remark, but Doctor Steele remained unconcerned.

"The murders are an unfortunate side effect," he replied. "You see, Ngila was only following the instincts of primitive man. Any anthropologist will tell you our progenitors were violent beings. They engaged in murder and cannibalism in an attempt to survive."

"What are you saying, Steele? Is this creature you've experimented on a man or a beast?"

"Ngila is still in the process of adapting and even evolving, doctor. Now do you understand the importance of the study?"

Hearing the remark, I stepped into the light. "Evolving into what, doctor?" I asked.

"I see you brought our friend Mr. Stone along, Quant. Very noble of you. As to the answer to your inquiry, Mr. Stone, I explained to you that Ngila is a part of one of our most ambitious studies in understanding the human genome. You see, as difficult as it might be to comprehend, Ngila is evolving into a modern human being. Along with his offspring, Ngila will guide us down the evolutionary path until we discover the true nature of the human species."

"And just exactly what is Ngila?"

"I would say he is currently equivalent to a man who lived more than four million years ago, Mr. Stone."

"Why, you mean, the missing link," I gasped.

Chapter Nineteen
The Missing Link

"The missing link," the supposed creature representing the transition from monkeys or apes to modern man, may have been found at a dig site near Barcelona in Spain in November of 2004. The 13-million-year-old partial skeleton may be the last probable common ancestor to humans and great apes, according to researchers. The creature had a body like an ape, fingers like a chimp and the upright posture of human beings. The new genus and species is called, Pierolapithecus catalaunicus.

The specimen found by researchers, headed by Salvador Moya-Sola, was probably a male, a fruit-eater and slightly smaller than a chimpanzee. One of the most complete ape skeletons from the Miocene Epoch (which took place about 22 to 5.5 million years ago), the find included parts of the skull, ribcage, spine, hands and feet, and other bones.

Scientists say the creature lived after the split from the lesser apes, but before the great apes evolved into orangutans, gorillas, chimps, and human beings. The living great apes are thought to have split from the lesser apes, such as gibbons and siamangs, about 14 million to 16 million years ago.

The creature that was found didn't knuckle walk on four limbs like a chimp and didn't swing through the trees with curved fingers like an orangutan. Its ribcage, lower spine and wrist reveal specialized climbing abilities, however, that link it with modern great apes. And the trunk was upright with a shaped chest and shoulder blades holding to a certain position on the back.

Whether the creature was "the missing link," researchers wouldn't say. According to co-author Meike Kohler, the phrase "missing link" is a very old concept and researchers prefer to avoid using it.

The term, "missing link," simply describes a transitional form that connects an earlier species to a later one, or two different species to an earlier ancestor. It is a creature that would include features common to both species.

For example, if a fossil had feathers like a modern bird and the bony tail and teeth of a dinosaur, that creature would be considered a missing link between dinosaurs and birds.

The lobe-finned fish Eusthenopteron is a link to land-dwelling amphibians. Fossils of feathered dinosaurs in China indicate a connection to modern birds, while amphibian fossils connect them to modern fish.

When talking about "the missing link," however, one is commonly referring to the creature that was the evolutionary transition from the earlier manlike apes to modern human beings.

Scientists still contend that the concept grew from a misunderstanding of Charles Darwin's writings that humans were direct descendants of present-day apes. To support this theory, the search began for fossil ape-men, such as *Homo erectus*, and the so-called "Piltdown man," which was later proven to be a hoax. The modern Khoikhoi, also known as the Hottentots, of southern Africa were also mistakenly suggested as the missing link when they were first discovered. According to many scientists, however, man and the present-day apes are related only through common ancestors, not direct descent.

One of these ancestors of human beings, however, is thought to be the Australopithecine, which was discovered in South Africa, and is regarded as an ape with manlike features of skull, teeth, and posture. They were later recognized as that crucial phase in human evolution when the body posture had become erect, but the brain was no bigger than that of living apes.

The first specimen of the creature was discovered in 1924 at Taungs in Botswana. It was then analyzed in a paper in 1925 by Raymond

Dart, then a young professor of anatomy in Johannesburg, who described the many apelike features of the skull, such as a small brain size, but also pointed out many of its manlike qualities. He proposed the species be placed in a grouping halfway between hominids, or the family of humans, and apes. He later examined the teeth of the specimen in more detail and became convinced that the subfamily *Australopithecus africanus* was actually a hominid or an ancestor of human beings.

About ten years later, Robert Broom, a South African paleontologist, discovered a second site in Sterkfontein valley, thirty miles west of Johannesburg. The site was rich in jaws, teeth, skulls, and other skeletal remains that were estimated to date back to the early Pleistocene epoch. This was the period of time characterized by the spread of glacial ice and eventually, the appearance of modern human beings.

Some of the interesting finds at Sterkfontein were the deep notches in the thighbones of some of the skeletal remains. This, scientists surmised, indicated a full extension of the knee in walking, a human trait.

There was also evidence that the creature hunted and was quite good at it. This conclusion was somewhat based on the discovery that baboons made up a portion of his food.

Later discoveries of the creature were made at a site about two hundred miles north of Johannesburg, and in the bed of the Olduvai Gorge in Tanganyika. The Leakeys, who discovered the site, found an almost complete adult Australopithecine skull. They reported a contrast between the front and back teeth and that the skull was accompanied by stone implements.

The significance of the australopithecine finding was that it gave substantial support to Charles Darwin's theory that man evolved and that he probably first came from Africa. *Australopithecus africanus* is believed to have later evolved into a larger-brained species known as *Homo habilis*. About 1.7 million years ago, the species developed further into *Homo erectus*. It was about five hundred thousand years ago that the species evolved into our own species of *Homo sapiens* or "the wise man." Scientists say our ancestors, however, had thicker skulls and brow ridges than we do today.

It's all part of the theory of evolution, which states that evidence shows current species of life evolved over time from earlier forms and that natural selection determined which species survived. Many, however, reject this theory in favor of creationism, which credits a supreme being or deity for creating human beings and other species. Many creationists now favor the term, "intelligent design," saying it promotes the idea that life is too complex to have developed without a creator. Many who dispute the theory of evolution take issue with the concept that humans are descended from "lesser creatures." They prefer that human beings are detached from Nature, and were created by a God. According to survey results, many people in the United States feel that way.

Half of the Americans responding in a nationwide poll taken at the beginning of the twenty-first century said the theory of evolution was "far from being proven scientifically." Sixty-eight percent said it was possible to believe in evolution while also believing a God created humans and guided their development.

According to the poll, conducted by a Danbury, Connecticut polling and research firm, most Americans thought creationism should be taught along with the theory of evolution. Although eighty-three percent supported the teaching of evolution, seventy-nine percent said creationism should also be taught in public schools.

The debate over teaching evolution first generated controversy in 1925, when John T. Scopes was charged with violating Tennessee law for teaching Darwin's theory in high school. His conviction and one hundred dollar fine were later overturned, but the debate continued. At the end of the twentieth century, the Kansas school board voted to remove references to evolution from state education standards.

The U.S. Supreme Court ruled in 1987 that creationism was a religious belief that couldn't be taught in public schools along with evolution.

The debate continued into the twenty-first century. In Kansas, debate over how evolution should be taught in public schools took place. The case against evolution was organized by advocates of intelligent design, a theory many scientists think is a form of creationism, prompting one Kansas Board of Education member to call evolution an "age-old fairy tale." Many favored the Bible, which does not offer a shred of evidence for any of its statements.

In Georgia, the education chief tried to take the word "evolution" out of the state's science curriculum. Then a suburban Atlanta county was taken to federal court over textbook stickers that call evolution "a theory, not a fact." The lawsuit contends that the constitutional separation of church and state was violated when Cobb County school officials placed the stickers in high school biology books in 2002 thereby promoting religion. The stickers say evolution should be "critically considered."

Kansas Schools Superintendent Kathy Cox then suggested the word "evolution" be dropped from the new science curriculum in favor of "changes over time." High school teachers worried students could be hurt when seeking admission to colleges.

Cobb County officials said they put the disclaimers in the books after more than 2,000 parents complained creationism, or other rival ideas, were not being presented along with evolution.

The sticker reads, "This textbook contains material on evolution. Evolution is a theory, not a fact, regarding the origin of living things. This material should be approached with an open mind, studied carefully and critically considered."

A lawyer for the school district said the sticker was meant to "encourage critical thinking" and did not imply that evolution was wrong. Many of the parents said the sticker was to emphasize that religious-based ideas weren't being mentioned, such as intelligent design.

In Grantsburg, Wisconsin, the city's school board revised its science curriculum to allow the teaching of creationism. The superintendent of the district of 1,000 students in northwest Wisconsin said the curriculum shouldn't include "just one scientific theory."

More than 300 biology and religious studies faculty members urged the Grantsburg board to reverse the policy. Evolution must be taught under Wisconsin law, but school districts are allowed to create their own curricular standards.

Meanwhile, in November of 2004, the Dover Area School Board in Pennsylvania voted to require the teaching of alternative theories to evolution, including intelligent design.

In March of 2004, the Ohio Board of Education approved a lesson plan than seemed to allow the teaching of creationism.

In the meantime, at the end of the twentieth century and the beginning of the twenty-first century, additional archeological findings included the discovery of a 1.5-million-year-old to two-million-year-old skull of a female *Paranthropus robustus*, a relative of early human beings.

Scientists said the hominid was a vegetarian who may have used bone tools. It became extinct about a million years ago, not being able to compete with early humans.

The skull was found twenty miles northwest of Johannesburg in an excavation site nicknamed "The Cradle of Humankind."

In the former Soviet republic of Georgia, skulls were found dating back 1.7 million years possibly demonstrating the migration of the first pre-humans out of Africa and into Europe.

The skulls resembled those of early humans who lived in East Africa at about the same time. The species of hominid, called *Homo ergaster*, lived sometime between *Homo habilis* and *Homo erectus*.

A fossilized partial skeleton of a baboon-sized ape that lived in East Africa about fifteen million years ago and was probably one of the first primates to leave the trees and live on the ground was also discovered in north central Kenya. The new ape genus, which scientists said was probably an evolutionary dead end, was dubbed, Equatorius.

Although the creature disappeared millions of years ago, it was seen as an example of a poorly understood era which scientists called "the golden age of ape evolution." During the Miocene Epoch, as many as 100 different ape species spread throughout the Old World, from France to China in Eurasia and from Kenya to Namibia in Africa.

A new species of human-like creatures who used stone tools and probably lived more than 2.5 million years ago was found in Ethiopia which scientists hoped could be the link between the genus *Homo*, which includes modern human beings, and its predecessor, *Australopithecus*.

The species, named *Australopithecus garhi*, had large teeth and a projecting face, and were similar to the well-known fossil Lucy. The importance of the discovery was that an antelope jaw and other animal bones were found near the skeleton, leading scientists to conclude that this may be the earliest known use of tools to butcher animals.

Other discoveries were also made including fossil fragments found in Ethiopia that were believed to belong to the oldest human ancestors, who probably lived millions of years ago.

Then there were the skull fragments of *Homo erectus* found on the island of Java that were estimated to be about 1.8 million years old. Another fossil find was uncovered in Ethiopia that supported the existence of the early apelike human ancestor, *Australopithecus afarensis*.

Meanwhile, Raymond Dart in an essay entitled, "The Predatory

Transition from Ape to Man," described the violence, including murder and cannibalism, which characterized early man.

This violence, he wrote, included seizing living creatures, including their fellow beings, battering them to death, tearing apart their bodies, dismembering them limb from limb, and then drinking their blood and devouring their flesh.

These creatures, which eventually evolved into modern human beings, were products of evolution, a theory scientists believe is as certain as the roundness of the Earth, the motions of the planets, and the molecular composition of matter. Darwin's nineteenth century theory was continually supported throughout the twentieth century by biological disciplines, such as genetics, biochemistry, physiology, and molecular biology. It was believed evolutionary changes through the centuries were stored in the DNA and proteins of living things and that only a method of obtaining the information was needed.

This became one of the main goals of the genome project, and the major objective of the Project Dawning study organized by Biocea Systems and Doctor Luther Steele.

Chapter Twenty
Hudge Stone

"Darwin was correct, my friends, life is based upon survival of the fittest," said Doctor Steele. "The notion that favorable variations within organisms results in some organisms having a competitive advantage over other organisms has been confirmed. Just look at Ngila. Why, Malthus would be ecstatic. Here, at last, is the living proof to support any theory dealing with evolution and the survival of the strong. My broad-shouldered friend here has flourished. Don't you see, doctor? It is exactly why I chose Ngila to continue the experiments. He was the strongest among our subjects, the one with the will to survive. Just look at him. He is the living example of what natural selection is supposed to be. My God, the implications are astounding."

"But what did he evolve from?" I asked.

"That is unimportant, Mr. Stone. At this point, he is a man. He is everything a man ever was. He even talks. Do you realize what that means? My God, not even the Neanderthals could talk. I couldn't even believe it at first. It was absolutely extraordinary, but somehow the evolutionary process caused him to develop the nerve complex needed to control the subtle and varied movement of the tongue required for speech. Yes, a developed hypoglossal canal. That, and of course, the FOXP2 gene. It caused the development of his larynx beyond our wildest expectations.

Yes, gentlemen, he is a man. You may call him a monster, but don't you see? The monster is us!"

Ngila sneered at the remark. "I am a man," he said in a throaty grunt.

"A man, a man," murmured Doctor Steele. "Why should you care what they think? They have no idea what momentous strides you've taken to secure your place in the species. If only you knew what you so want to be a part of, my friend." He shook his head and began examining the bullet wound once again.

"Man is actually a very frail creature, my friend, open to hatreds and temptations that cause him to disdain the needs of other creatures on the planet. Isn't that right, gentlemen? A violent creature, driven by vanity and the lust for power, whose success depends solely on his ability to think. I imagine you are learning this is true, my friend, for you see you're more a man than you know. You are what man was, and we are your progeny. Yes, I dare say, you are more a man than you know."

"Ngila a man."

"And so you are. You have killed indiscriminately, only considering your own thirst for blood. You have torn the flesh from your brother in a desperate attempt to satiate your belligerent soul. When the madness of lust enveloped you, you captured a woman to fulfill your primitive sexual needs. Yes, Ngila, you are a man. You are everything man was meant to be ever since Cain murdered his brother and perpetuated the human race. How could anyone know the experiments would be such a success? A success, gentlemen. To actually see our ancestors in the flesh, the very link between man and beast…the beast that is man."

"But how?" I asked.

"I will answer that in a moment, Mr. Stone. But right now Ngila needs some rest."

With Doctor Steele's help, Ngila leaned back upon the operating table. When he was sufficiently comfortable, Doctor Steele led Doctor Quant and I out of the room, and back into the hallway. In a few moments, we were back inside the room containing the gray sofa.

"Quite incredible," said Doctor Quant with a shake of his head.

"But how is it possible?" I asked.

"You see, Mr. Stone, we were forced to pursue alternative methods to attain the stated goal," Doctor Steele began. "We had found evolution is not as long a process as previously thought. It can actually occur over just a few years, as incredible as that sounds. We based our original theories on the remarkably rapid evolution in bacteria, snails, moths, and a host of other creatures. We decided it was actually possible in larger animals, even mammals. It is known in scientific circles as directed evolution, and began as a way to speed up evolution in test tubes. You see, using various laboratory methods, genes are manipulated, pressured, redesigned, you might say, to mutate in thousands of ways, accomplishing in days or weeks what can take Nature years. For example, it took decades for certain bacteria to evolve to resist antibiotics, but we can create new super germs to test new antibiotics in a matter of days. Farmers, Mr. Stone, are already using the method to breed better animals and plants, and we have incorporated it into simulating evolutionary growth.

"You see, it all has to do with our growing knowledge of genes, the essential foundation of life. Experimenting with organisms such as the bacterium Mycoplasma genitallium, we have discovered the minimal set of genes that a species would need to live and replicate itself. Don't you understand the implications? Why, we're on the verge of creating life itself! I dare say, the human body is far more complicated than bacteria, with about 25,000 genes, but still we have already identified them and are beginning to understand their biological function. Don't you see? Ngila is just the tip of the iceberg. We soon will no longer be dependent upon the whims of Nature, but will be able to create life in the laboratory, in a mere test tube. In this very building, we are in the process of creating many Ngilas, utilizing human embryo cells, all in various stages of evolutionary development. Yes, my friends, Cro-Magnons, Neanderthals, *Homo erectus*, Australopithecines, all with the manipulation of both human and anthropoid genes. Before long, we will have a complete understanding of the human species and its origins. I dare say, more than we ever could have hoped when Project Dawning began all those years ago.

"But, you see, even with our biological knowledge, we must test our theories in the world at large to verify our stated beliefs. Medical solutions are not enough. Environment is equally important."

"Is that the reason you brought Ngila to New York?" I asked.

"Well, you see, Mr. Stone, we had already done statistical studies that proved environment was extremely important in determining a person's IQ. Ngila was only familiar with the rain forests of the Congo. I decided he needed a modern environment in order to prompt his intellect to develop to its full potential. And New York City was the perfect place to bring about this development."

"So you let a known killer roam around the streets of New York in the interests of science?"

"It was the only way to know whether our scientific theories were correct. And I would have to say they were. As a result, Ngila began to think and talk in a more civilized manner. You see, according to Locke, all knowledge is derived from experience. Yes, we are born almost blank slates filled by ideas that come from experience of the senses. We applied this philosophical theory to Ngila and found it to be true. Due to his experiences in the city, Ngila began formulating ideas. Yes, and even reflecting upon them."

"Incredible," murmured Doctor Quant.

"Yes, Quant understands. There is so much we can learn from Ngila and the others who will follow, everything from the intricacies of the human mind to the eradication of disease. Why, a study of Ngila and the others could lead to an explanation of the violent tendencies of human beings and how to control them. They could help unlock the secrets of genetics, thereby eradicating abnormalities of any kind. And, of course, provide an understanding of the will to survive. You see, I didn't extinguish his thirst for survival. Why, the possibilities for study are boundless. Think of it, doctor, a talking remnant of our past."

"A remnant of our violent past, doctor," I said.

"Yes, so much the better," replied Doctor Steele. "He is a reflection of man's darker side at this point, Mr. Stone — a meat-eater, just as our early ancestors were. Apes who decided eating plants were not enough to survive, and thereby caused the leap which brought about the human being as we know him today."

"So then Ngila began life as an ape," I suggested.

"Not an ordinary ape, Mr. Stone. You see, through the use of genetic engineering and biotechnology, Ngila's genes were manipulated, spliced, and transplanted along with human genes, and therefore, human DNA. The whole process brought about something far different than an ordinary ape. Why, his genes have been combined with those of a human being. I dare say, he is as much a man as any creature who walked the earth more than four million years ago."

"Extraordinary," said Doctor Quant.

"I quite agree, doctor, which is why I will not allow anything to happen to Ngila. You see, the experiment is not yet completed. When I feel Ngila has subjugated his violent tendencies, it is my intention to exhibit him before my scientific colleagues. They will be able to examine him and conclude that the experiment was a success. In the meantime, gentlemen, I'm afraid I have no choice but to confine you to this room. I'm sure you understand it is imperative to keep the experiment a secret until Ngila is ready. I've already had to have others killed to maintain that secret. I will allow no one to interfere until the time arrives when I can reveal Ngila to the world."

"It's not that simple, doctor. You see, the police have already been informed of Ngila's whereabouts, and at this moment, are probably on their way here."

"I'm fully aware of that fact, Mr. Stone. It's exactly why I must leave you now, and prepare for their arrival. They've already shot Ngila, and I don't intend for him to be injured any further. It was nice seeing you again, doctor. You can take comfort in the fact that the experiments were a success. I hope you are pleased."

Doctor Steele then turned, stepped out of the room, and locked the door behind him.

"How do we get out this time?" I asked, turning toward Doctor Quant.

"I really can't say," murmured Doctor Quant. "But if I wasn't so opposed to the method, I would have to admit the experiments were truly a success. It's unfortunate the creature is such a ruthless killer. We could've learned so much."

"But he was an ape. How is that possible?"

"It only proves that man was once a beast, Mr. Stone. I'm beginning to think that creature could be valuable after all. If only I could perform some tests on him to see just how much he's evolved. Why, it's even possible he may have the ability to produce tools."

"He may be able to make tools, doctor, but he's also shown the ability to kill."

"But don't you see? That creature is the missing link between man and beast. By God, he can talk. Think of what we can learn from him. I'm beginning to understand Steele's enthusiasm. I hope the police will consider capturing him alive. To lose such a creature would be quite injurious to the cause of science."

"Then you believe it's all true? Project Dawning was a success?"

"I certainly do, Mr. Stone. When I left the project, we hadn't even begun experimenting with mixing the ape genes with those of a human being. And with the change of environment, Doctor Steele has done much to speed up the process. Taking into consideration the scientific advances we've made in the past few years, I think the success of the experiments is not that surprising. It will surely be proven that the greatest discovery of the twentieth century was the structure of DNA. And now, with our understanding of genes, anything is possible."

"What do you mean, doctor?"

"Well, Mr. Stone, I refer to other similar experiments going on even as we speak. For instance, at a top-secret farm hidden somewhere in the Northeast, scientists are growing pigs whose DNA have been altered with human genes. They plan to use the pigs in the treatment of human organ failures, spinal cord injuries, and illnesses such as Parkinson's disease. The idea is to transplant the animal parts in humans and somehow prevent the human body from rejecting the organs.

"The first altered pigs, created with the help of researchers at Virginia Tech in the early 1990s, contained a human gene called CD-59. This grafted gene was supposed to trick the human body's immune system into believing the pig parts were human. The major breakthrough came when scientists figured out a way to alter a sugar-like molecule in the pig cells so that human antibodies wouldn't recognize them as foreign. Thus far, the process has worked. In fact, scientists have already transplanted brain cells from the altered pigs into rodents who suffer from a syndrome similar to Parkinson's. The transplanted cells not only survived, but became neurotransmitters in the animals' brains and helped correct the tremors. Next, they experimented on baboons and, so far, those experiments have also been successful. Researchers say that if all goes well, humans will soon be able to receive permanent organ transplants from pigs.

"Now, I ask you, Mr. Stone, how are these experiments much different than those that produced Ngila. In fact, creatures such as Ngila would be perfect subjects to use for human transplants, including the use of their brain and spinal cells to eradicate a whole host of diseases and maladies. There's no doubt about it, our understanding of genes is changing so many aspects of medicine, including how these genes trigger many diseases such as cancer."

"But what will religious leaders, animal rights activists, and others say about the possibility of manipulating life?"

"They'd complain until these scientific breakthroughs helped them or their loved ones. Animals have always been essential in helping to eradicate human disease. I don't hear any complaints when a scientific discovery ends up saving millions of human lives."

"Yes, doctor, but…"

"Why, Mr. Stone, the possibilities are endless. Do you realize we are currently experimenting with the genetic engineering of plants and animals? Why, in the years ahead, there will be gene-engineered potatoes, cotton, grains, and trees. And why not? Plants and animals are easily genetically manipulated to speed their growth and make them more resistant to disease.

"Why, creatures such as Ngila, which depend upon the fusing of human and animal cells, will have all kinds of applications and could even be used for the cloning of cells to help create human replacement organs. Why not? The creatures are almost human themselves.

"An Edinburgh company utilizes the technique in fusing sheep cells with modified sheep eggs to produce transgenic offspring. The technique, which is also being used on mice, allows scientists to suppress unwanted genes and introduce modifications. This will lead to the shutting down of certain genes that can cause allergies or disease. It will also be used in gene therapy in humans in which genes are taken from a patient, modified, and then replaced."

"Is all this possible?"

"They are taking place as we speak, Mr. Stone. There are great changes ahead, I can tell you that. And Project Dawning is only a small part of it. One look at that creature will tell you that I am right."

"But he has killed," I said.

"Yes, human in every way. Doctor Steele is correct, he is the beast that is man."

I was about to reply when a loud noise resounded through the hallway. There was a great crash and then the tramping of many feet for several moments, until suddenly, they halted in front of the large black door. We could hear voices shouting in great alarm, and then another crash, and the large black door flew open.

"Oh, Hudge!" cried Sandra, accompanied by several police officers. She hurried toward me and fell into my arms. "Thank God, you're all right."

"What about Doctor Steele and Ngila?" I asked.

"Yes, be careful with that creature," interjected Doctor Quant. "He is very valuable to the future of mankind."

A police officer looked at him with a shake of his head. "Sorry, doctor, but there's nobody else here."

Chapter Twenty-One
Doctor Luther Steele

This is the speech I intend to make to my scientific colleagues when introducing Ngila to the world:

Thank you for inviting me to speak today. It is an honor to be among a distinguished group of colleagues who recognize the importance of seeking progress for humanity with the advances in technology.

The last few years have seen enormous scientific advancements that can help forge the next step in our own evolution. These developments will challenge our concept of what it means to be "human." Although human beings cannot be patented, there is still no legal definition of a "human being." The next several decades will surely test the law in this regard.

In Greek mythology, the chimera was part lion, part goat, part dragon, which was eventually slain by the hero Bellerophon. In modern day biology, a chimera is a genetically engineered creature created from the DNA of different species. This is not any longer science fiction, but scientific fact. Through the process of DNA recombinant research, we are now able to splice genes together from different species that would normally not be able to mate. The benefits to the human race are immeasurable. Let me briefly outline some of these benefits.

First of all, Esmail Zanjani, a researcher at the University of Nevada at Reno, has been growing human livers in sheep. He does this by injecting into growing sheep fetuses either adult stem cells derived from bone marrow, or embryonic stem cells from approved stem cell colonies. The human cells were integrated into the organism and proliferated. Because of such research, it seems possible to grow inside animals human cells from which tissues and organs can be used for transplants into people.

A person's bone marrow stem cells can be injected into a fetal sheep, and then, a few weeks later would be born with a liver or some other organ made up chiefly of your cells. The new organ would be perfectly matched to your body, your immune system eliminating the lamb's liver cells.

And that's not all. Researcher J. Michael Bedford reported in 1977 that human sperm could penetrate the outer membranes of gibbon eggs. The mixing of human and animal genes was at hand. The benefits again are enormous.

At Stanford University's Institute of Cancer/Stem Cell Biology and Medicine in California, mice have been created with brains that are about one percent human.

There are now experiments taking place in which the mice have 100 percent human brains. This is done by injecting human neurons into the brains of embryonic mice. The result? A detailed study of the brain which will lead to treating diseases like Alzheimer's or Parkinson's disease.

And what about, as suggested by Bioethicist Joseph Fletcher, the creation of parahumans, human and animal hybrids that can be used to do dangerous and demeaning jobs. Is it any different from training dolphins to find underwater explosives, or using dogs to sniff out dangerous criminals and drugs?

Why, the possibilities are endless. We would be able to give an animal the ability to walk upright on two legs and even to talk. That's right, through the use of the FOXP2 gene, animals could be given the ability to talk and help us unlock the mysteries of illness and disease. It is not as unlikely as you think. The proteins produced by the FOXP2 gene in humans differs by only two amino acids from the proteins produced by the FOXP2 gene in chimpanzees, gorillas, and orangutans.

The benefits to the human race could not be calculated. Such products of the laboratory could be used for testing drugs to cure or prevent various human brain diseases. They could also be used to help people overcome infertility.

Bone marrow stem cells from an infertile woman or man could be injected into a fetal mouse, where they could then become gamete-producing cells, and then could be harvested from the mice to produce a human child. Yes, that's right.

The possibilities are endless. Through genetic engineering, there are so many illnesses, such as diabetes, that can be conquered with the insertion or removal of genes in the right places. And with our knowledge of the human genome, people can be genetically engineered to regenerate limbs, spine, and the brain. But it doesn't stop there. People can be made stronger, faster, smarter, have better reaction time, and survive underwater longer. If Nature has created it, it is then possible to incorporate it into the human body.

For example, if you wanted to regrow something, you find a creature that can do this in Nature. The newt is a good example. Then after isolating the genes that make that happen, you make the changes to the human body. This can be done by transferring the whole block of genes to the person's body. They are then incorporated into the human body and invade the host cells, inserting themselves into the genes of the cells. The product of this is a human being who can regrow limbs and other body parts. Think of it.

How do I know that this is all possible? To answer that question, I have brought along Ngila. He is a perfect example of the possibilities of genetic engineering. By fusing the cells of a human being and gorilla, I have created man's earliest progenitor, the missing link!

Through the study of Ngila and others like him, the human race will learn about its origins, and in doing so, find the origins of many illnesses and diseases. We will be able to study human development through the ages, and finally come to understand the workings of our society and brains. Yes, Ngila is our future, ladies and gentlemen, a future in which human beings become the supreme rulers of their earthly domain.

As an intelligent transgenic creature, Ngila is the first of the parahumans who can help us take control of our planet. Similar creatures will be perfect for any dangerous and demeaning job we may have.

As you can see, the value of these creatures is inestimable in helping the human race understand itself and the planet. I hope all of you will take the time to meet and study Ngila. I'm sure you will soon find that what I say is irrefutable. In the name of a better future for all, I thank you for your attention.

Chapter Twenty-Two
Hudge Stone

"Steele and the creature are gone?" asked Doctor Quant incredulously. "But we must find them. It's essential that we examine that creature and establish a new phase of Project Dawning."

"Project Dawning?" asked one of the officers.

"It was a government program that had been studying the origins of the human race that's now being run by Biocea," I explained.

"Yes, and that creature that was here is part of that program," said Doctor Quant. "We must find him before he does any more damage."

"Well, whoever was here left the building before we arrived," replied the officer. "And as far as a creature running around, that wouldn't be the monster we've been searching for, would it?"

"The same," I nodded. "But, you see, he's actually a primitive man."

"A what?" said the officer with a frown. "Come on, Stone, is this some sort of publicity stunt dreamed up by your paper?"

"No, officer, they're telling the truth," said Sandra. "It's the monster just as I explained to you."

"Well, we'll clear this up soon enough," he said. "We have officers checking the entire building. There's got to be someone here who knows what the hell is going on."

"At least, you're all right," said Sandra, stroking her hand across my cheek. "But you didn't find Molly?"

"We didn't have time," I replied. "We had just spoken with Doctor Steele when he locked us in this room again. And now they're gone."

"Yes, but now we know the secret of that creature," said Doctor Quant. "If only they can find him so that we can study him in an appropriate manner."

Doctor Quant had just finished speaking when they heard footsteps and voices in the hallway. Then several officers entered the room.

"We found someone," one of them said. "In an upstairs laboratory."

"Thank God," exclaimed Doctor Quant. "Is it Doctor Steele?"

"I don't know," said the officer. "He said he was working late."

Another officer soon entered the room holding a balding man in his thirties by the arm. When he stepped into the light, Doctor Quant looked at him and was immediately crestfallen.

"That's not him," he said. "Didn't you find anybody else?"

The officer shook his head. "He's the only one we found in the building."

"Do you know where Doctor Steele went?" asked Doctor Quant.

The man stared at the crowd surrounding him and began to stammer. "I…I don't know anything about Doctor Steele," he replied. "He only comes here once in a while to check up on things and to inquire about the progress of our work."

"That's a lie!" shouted Doctor Quant.

The man glanced at the officers and grimaced. "I…I swear, Doctor Steele has not been in the building all day."

"But we talked to him, here, only a few minutes ago," I argued.

"That's impossible," replied the man. "Doctor Steele said he wouldn't be back until next week."

"And I suppose you know nothing about that creature, either," said Doctor Quant.

"Cr…Creature? Why, we have all kinds of creatures here. What creature are you referring to?"

"You damn well know what creature I'm referring to," roared Doctor Quant. "Now I don't know who put you up to this, but you better start telling the truth if you know what's good for you."

The man turned toward the officers. "Is he threatening me?" he asked.

One of the officers put his arms around the man and attempted to calm him. "Now, come on, this is getting us nowhere," he said. "I suggest we question this man in private."

"But don't you see, officers? This man is trying to protect Doctor Steele. Nothing he has said is even close to the truth."

"Doctor Quant is right," I said. "The monster is on the loose, and this man is trying to tell us he doesn't even exist."

"Mo…Monster?" stammered the man. "Really, officers, there are no monsters here, I can assure you. This is a medical research building, not a medieval castle. Whatever experiments we perform, we do in the interest of saving human lives. You may look if you like, but you won't find any monsters here."

"Can't you see he's lying?" I replied.

"Well, we did get a report of the monster being shot and headed in this direction," said one of the officers. "You know nothing about that?"

"There are no monsters here, officer, although I admit it would be quite a research project. If you look around, you will find monkeys, rats, and other assorted animals, but definitely not any monsters. Why, it's utterly absurd."

The officers looked at Doctor Quant, who shook his head in disgust. "He is not a monster, I will agree," he finally said. "But an ape that has been genetically altered with human DNA into the missing link, the evolutionary relative of both man and beast."

"Why, it's absurd. First, there are monsters running around and now it's a missing link? Officers, do you really take these gentlemen seriously?"

"I'm beginning to wonder," said one of the officers. "Do you really expect us to believe the missing link is running around somewhere in this city? Why, it's the most ridiculous thing I ever heard."

"Precisely, officer. Why, even if those creatures did exist, they haven't walked the earth in hundreds of thousands of years, maybe even millions. And to suggest that one of these creatures was somehow magically produced by this company is, indeed, quite absurd. But don't take my word for it, feel free to look around."

"Then why were we held in this room against our will?" I argued.

"I...I imagine one of our technicians caught them snooping around and when they were told to leave, they refused, babbling about some missing link on the loose. Identified as trespassers, they were placed in this room until the proper authorities could be called to sort it all out. You understand, officers, we don't want any trouble."

"I can understand that," said one of the officers. "Well, Stone, what do you have to say about all this?"

I glanced at Doctor Quant, who seemed to be baffled as to what to say, and then at Sandra, who lovingly caressed my arm. "We may have been trespassing," I finally said, "but there was a damned good reason for it. We saw Ngila, that's the monster's name, enter through the back door and we followed him inside. It appeared as if he had been shot in the arm."

"Re...Really, officers, I never heard such a story in all my life," stammered the man. "Why, you can search the entire building. We have no one here who has been shot."

"But you said the monster had been shot, officer," I said. "Well, apparently he came back here. Doctor Steele was the one who removed the bullet."

"That's only because he heard you talking about it. As I said, Doctor Steele hasn't been here all day."

"And I still say he's lying," fumed Doctor Quant. "That creature was here, he had a bullet wound, and I personally saw Doctor Steele remove that bullet. We even talked to him before he locked us in this room."

"Quite absurd."

"You can deny it if you like, but I'm going back to my newspaper and write a story about all this, I can tell you that," I said. "No one is going to convince me I didn't see what I saw, and hear what I heard." I then pulled from my pocket my reporter's notebook, which was filled with Doctor Steele's quotes. "Now are you going to tell me I imagined all this?"

I then handed the notebook to one of the officers, who began perusing the pages. "Okay, Stone, it's obvious you talked to someone who you believed was Doctor Steele. I'm going to call it in and put out an alert on this Steele character. We'll get to the bottom of this eventually."

"I still plan on writing a story. I have quotes from Doctor Steele, Doctor Quant, and even Ngila himself. There's no doubt in my mind that what they told me is true."

"Y…You can print it if you like, but as far as I'm concerned, it's a pack of lies. I didn't realize your paper printed fiction."

"I'll add your denial to the story," said Stone. "What about you, officer, is the police department also going to issue a denial?"

"We have nothing to say until the investigation is completed, Stone. We don't even know who or what we're looking for. All I know is that an officer reported the monster being shot in the park last night. You say he showed up here today. Well, all right, we're going to keep searching. Until that time, we have no comment."

It was then I noticed an officer standing near the doorway who looked familiar. "Wait a minute, isn't that Officer Bombeck? Well, he saw the monster. He can tell you we're not dreaming all of this."

Everyone turned to look at the officer, who sheepishly bowed his head. "I don't know what you're talking about," he mumbled. "I never saw any monster."

"But you were there on that rooftop when we saw him," I argued. "I even remember the look on your face when we first spotted him."

"Reporters," snorted Bombeck. "They're supposed to make their living knowing the facts, and they always get it wrong or end up just making it up."

I stared at him in disbelief. "Now you're telling me you don't know anything about any monster? What's going on here? Well, I saw him I can tell you that. And Doctor Quant can verify it."

I turned to Doctor Quant, who patted me on the back. "Don't worry, my friend, I won't betray you. The problem is if they don't believe us, we may never find the creature. And that is very unfortunate."

"Well, I saw him, too," Sandra interjected. "He abducted me and told me he loved me. I will never forget that. And then he brought me to this very room. And then there was a pregnant woman, who said she was carrying the monster's baby, who helped us escape. It's all true, officers, and hopefully, we find them soon and put an end to all of this."

Some of the officers looked at each other and smiled in mocking disbelief. I noticed their reaction and became enraged.

"What do we have to do to prove to you that we saw what we saw?" I shouted.

Officer Bombeck, seeing my distress, stepped forward. "Maybe you can show us all the places you saw the monster so we could possibly find some physical evidence?"

I thought for a moment. "Well, he was in this room and then…"

"And Doctor Steele left that creature in the operating room," said Doctor Quant.

"Yes, that's it, the operating room!"

I turned and weaved my way through the officers. When I reached the dimly lit hallway, I hurried down the corridor. Several officers followed me until I halted in front of a gray door.

"Here it is!" I cried. "This is where Doctor Steele removed the bullet."

We opened the door and stepped inside. The room was totally empty.

"There must be something here to prove their existence," I said, beginning to search the room.

"You'd better let us take care of it," said one of the officers. "We don't want anything in here disturbed."

"But he was right here on this operating table. Doctor Steele took the bullet out and then he laid down…"

"All right, Mr. Stone, let us do our job."

I hung my head, and dejectedly walked toward the door. It was then I noticed something catch the light near the shadow of the operating table. I bent down and squinted into the shadow. After a moment, I bolted to attention.

"Here it is, officers," I shouted. "Thank God, here it is!"

There beneath the operating table, a small drop of blood lay spattered upon the floor.

Chapter Twenty-Three
New York Herald

THE MYSTERY OF THE MONSTER OF CENTRAL PARK REVEALED!

By Hudge Stone

The "Monster of Central Park" is actually a creation of the laboratory, a rampaging chimera that is half human and half gorilla.

That's the stunning revelation made by Doctor Luther Steele, responsible for creating the monster, in an exclusive interview with the *Herald*. In another exclusive interview, the *Herald* talked with — that's right, talked with — the monster himself, whose name is Ngila.

The monster, who is actually a genetically engineered creature with the DNA of both a human being and a gorilla which is called a chimera from Greek mythology, can talk thanks to a gene, FOXP2, that was inserted into his cells when he was created by Doctor Steele.

In a harrowing adventure in which this reporter was captured by Doctor Steele along with a woman named Sandra Barton, who was earlier abducted on the streets of Manhattan, the "Monster of Central

Park" was asked why he insists on killing the people of this city.

"Defending myself," was all the massive, bent figure would say.

When asked why he reportedly eats his victims or their brains, the monster simply said, "Must keep strong. People's spirits keep Ngila strong."

Although first thought to be a primitive tribesman from Africa, it was subsequently discovered, and confirmed by Doctor Steele, that the monster is actually part gorilla. His name, Ngila, is from the African Mbeti dialect and means gorilla.

Asked if it was wrong to kill, Ngila responded, "Does not man kill?" When explained to him that man usually kills for a reason, Ngila said, "Man kills when he wants to kill. He kills the animals without reason. He kills other men without reason. I am a man. Do not tell me it is wrong to kill."

Amazingly, the monster was coached by Doctor Steele, and speaks and understands English surprisingly well.

"I would say he (the monster) is currently equivalent to a man who lived more than four million years ago," said Doctor Steele.

This means, according to Doctor Steele, that Ngila, the "Monster of Central Park," is actually very much like the elusive missing link, the supposed creature that represents the transition from apes to modern human beings.

"Here, at last, is the living proof to support any theory dealing with evolution and the survival of the strong," explained Doctor Steele. "At this point, he is a man. He is everything a man ever was. He even talks."

And that, says Doctor Dekko Quant, a director of the human genome project and a participant in the so-called Project Dawning that produced Ngila, makes the monster very special.

"If I wasn't so opposed to the method, I would have to admit the experiments were truly a success," he said. "It's unfortunate the creature is such a ruthless killer. We could've learned so much."

And this is also apparently a side effect of the experiments — Ngila kills like our early human ancestors.

He also mates.

Sandra Barton was abducted for this very reason, and so was at least one other woman, Molly Rogers.

When asked about Miss Barton, the monster responded, "Ngila love her." Then he looked at Miss Barton and said, "You, mate."

Meanwhile, the police and those working at Doctor Steele's laboratory insist the monster doesn't exist.

"I don't know anything about Doctor Steele," said one lab worker. "He only comes here once in a while to check up on things and to inquire about the progress of our work."

This reporter, however, spoke with Doctor Steele inside the Biocea Systems laboratory only moments before.

The police also issued a denial, although they admitted receiving a report of the monster being shot in the arm only hours before.

"Well, we did get a report of the monster being shot and headed in this direction," said one police officer. He then added, for the time being, the police would have no comment. "We have nothing to say until the investigation is completed. We don't even know who or what we're looking for. All I know is that an officer reported the monster being shot in the park last night. We're going to keep searching. Until that time, we have no comment."

The problem is Doctor Steele and Ngila, the "Monster of Central Park," are missing. They disappeared after talking to this reporter, Doctor Quant, and Sandra Barton. Where they are headed, or where they are hiding, no one currently knows.

The experiments that produced Ngila were carried out in the African Congo, initially as part of the Human Genome Project. The completed international project was responsible for the mapping of the human genetic blueprint.

Another part of the project was supposed to investigate genes and inheritance through the centuries. This project later became a project funded by Biocea Systems, headed by Doctor Steele. It ended up in producing Ngila, the "Monster of Central Park."

-END-

Chapter Twenty-Four
Hudge Stone

I sat at my desk typing furiously. I wrote how I discovered the monster was actually a genetically altered remnant of man's past. I wrote about Project Dawning and the experiments seeking to influence his evolutionary growth through the use of human DNA and the manipulation of his genes. I explained how these experiments transformed the creature into a cannibalistic, meat-eating killer just like the early ancestors of the human race. Yes, and how the creature was then brought to New York City in the interests of civilizing his psyche. All this I included in my story, a lengthy account filled with startling revelations that were given credence through the quotes of Doctor Quant, Doctor Lido, and Doctor Steele. Why, even the monster himself! Besides, there were the genome project papers, filled with facts and figures supplied by none other than the government of the United States of America.

All this I included in my story. I even included the doubts expressed by the police department, the admission that a creature they thought to be the monster had been shot the night before inside Central Park, and the denials of police officers and the man on Biocea's staff that such a creature ever existed.

When I had completed my story, I glanced over to Sandra and Doctor Quant, who were sitting nearby.

"Do you think anybody will believe us?" I asked.

"They must, Mr. Stone, if we're ever to find that creature," replied Doctor Quant. "For all we know, he might be in another state by now."

"But it's so incredible, even to me. I mean, the missing link himself? Why, it's something those supermarket tabloids would publish. I mean, this is a reputable newspaper. A story like this is either going to earn me a Pulitzer Prize or a pink slip. If only we had a photograph, or other reliable eyewitnesses."

"You have us, Hudge," said Sandra. "And Doctor Quant is known around the world. People will believe him."

"Yes, I know, but if only the police had seen him this would all be very easy. I mean, even if that lab technician had admitted to the experiments, I wouldn't have any worries at all. But the problem is, we're the only ones who admit to seeing him. Everyone else in authority denies he exists."

"But there's the genome papers," said Doctor Quant. "No one will dispute such incontestable evidence. It traces the experiments to their very origins. And what about all the people who have seen him? They're all scared and confused, not knowing what's going on. Everyone thinks there's a monster on the loose, and you've got to tell them that they're right. That's why your story is so important, Mr. Stone. It will finally explain to people just who and what the monster is."

"If only they believe it, doctor."

"Don't worry, Mr. Stone, after your story is printed, they'll find the creature. Then there'll be no doubt of anything we've said. Once they find Doctor Steele, we'll be vindicated, you'll see. You might just win that Pulitzer Prize, after all."

"I sure hope so, doctor."

After a few moments, I glanced at my city editor, who was busy reading the story. "Are you going to run it?" I asked.

My editor looked up. "I don't see any reason not to," he replied. "As long as Doctor Quant backs you up and all your facts are correct, there should be no problem. It is quite incredible, though. But I don't think we'll have any problem selling any newspapers tomorrow."

"I'm happy to hear you say that," said Doctor Quant. "It's

imperative that as many people as possible read that story. It's the only way the police will take it seriously and finally do everything they can to find that creature."

"Is he really the missing link, doctor?" asked the editor.

"As close as scientifically possible," replied Doctor Quant. "You see, the experiments seem to have been a success."

"Amazing."

I waited for my editor to finish the story, and then grabbed my coat. "Let's get something to eat," I said to Doctor Quant and Sandra. "It's been one helluva long day."

We walked across the newsroom, opened a door, and made our way to the street. A full moon glared down from above as we strolled down the avenue. As we stepped into a restaurant, we resolved not to discuss the creature, Doctor Steele, or Project Dawning. Some time later, we finished our meal, glanced outside and noticed it was raining.

"Would you do me a favor, doctor, and make sure Sandra gets home safely?" I asked. "I've got to get some sleep."

"It would be my pleasure, Mr. Stone."

"Good, I think it would be best if we all meet at the newspaper tomorrow afternoon. We'll be able then to see what kind of reaction the story receives, and whether the police have any luck finding Doctor Steele."

"We'll be there, Mr. Stone." He glanced at Sandra, who had made her way to my side.

"Don't worry, Hudge, everything's going to work out," she said. She then reached up and kissed me. "See you tomorrow."

We stepped outside into the ragged chill of the falling rain, and after a few minutes, a cab pulled up to the curb. Sandra and Doctor Quant slipped inside as I watched them disappear amid the glaring lights and the enveloping darkness.

I then turned up the collar of my jacket, and sauntered down the street. When I reached the corner, I hailed a cab, and was soon heading back to my apartment. On the way, I thought about my story, and whether Doctor Steele would ever be found. The rain continued to patter against the cab window. I watched one of the drops skid across the glass and then vanish back into the night.

The next morning, I awoke and turned on the television. A man in a dark blue suit was in the midst of reading the news.

"According to the Herald report, the ape has been genetically altered and has evolved into the missing link, that legendary creature assumed to have existed between the anthropoid ape and man. Religious leaders have condemned the story as a fraud, while animal rights activists have attacked the experiments as 'inhumane."

I turned off the television and sighed. The accusations had already begun. I decided I would get dressed and return to the newspaper as soon as possible. It was obviously going to be a long day. I put on a black suit and red tie, carefully brushed my hair, and headed for the door.

A half-hour later, my cab pulled up in front of the *Herald* building. Protesters had already gathered on the sidewalk, and as I stepped out of the cab, I watched as they marched in two separate circles and held signs displaying their objections. I stood staring at one of the signs, which read, ADAM DIDN'T EAT BANANAS, and could hear them chanting, "Stop the cruelty now."

I moved slowly into the crowd of protesters, removing my notebook from my back pocket. I then approached a woman in a red blouse.

"I'm Hudge Stone of the *Herald*," I said. "What exactly didn't you like about the story?"

"Stone?" she repeated. "Why this is the man who wrote that blasphemous article."

I watched as the small group of people stopped marching. They turned to glare at me, and then slowly surrounded me.

"Damnation!" one of them shouted. "God created man in his own image. Are you saying God is an ape?"

"I never said anything of the kind," I replied. "I only reported the scientists involved believed the creature was evolving."

"Sheer nonsense," said a tall man with thinning hair, making his way through the crowd. "I'm the Reverend James Matthews, and I say those experiments were nothing more than an ordinary fraud."

The small knot of people cheered the statement, enthusiastically waving their signs in the air.

"You see, young man, the Bible tells us that God created man from the dust of the earth and that is what we shall always believe. There is no spark of the divine in an ape. That is the providence of man, and of mankind alone."

There was another cheer from the crowd, and I stepped back fearful they were about to charge.

"But what about Darwin, Malthus, Mendel, and the fields of archeology and anthropology?" I asked. "I mean the evidence of some form of evolution is enormous. Do you choose to ignore everything that science has learned?"

"Science can never explain why human beings are the only ones who have established a covenant with the Lord. Why are we the only ones who can think and speak?"

"But this creature can think and speak."

"An abomination created by the laboratory!" shouted the reverend. "Nothing more! We will be guided by the Lord, not the heresy of a few scientists!"

The crowd applauded once again, and the reverend turned toward them. "Heresy!" he shouted. "Heresy!"

While the chanting reached a feverish pitch, I quietly hurried to the other group of demonstrators.

"Stop the unethical treatment of animals," one of them shouted. He held a sign that read, PUT AN END TO THE CRUELTY.

I approached one of the women in the crowd and identified myself. "Well, sir," she said, "you failed to point out in your article the utter cruelty of these experiments upon another living being."

"But I said in the story that Doctor Quant left Project Dawning because he thought the experiments were cruel."

"That was only one scientist," said the woman. "What about everyone else working on that project? Didn't they realize the cruelty involved?"

"I think they would say it was the only way to attain the knowledge they were seeking. Knowledge that, in the future, could possibly save innumerable human lives."

"That's always the excuse. In the meantime, how much suffering do they cause? How many needless deaths?"

"What about all the things we could learn from Ngila? What about the medical advances he could possibly provide?"

"We don't need to learn those things if it means performing inhumane experiments," she replied.

I nodded, and wrote the woman's words down in my notebook. I then watched as the woman turned back toward her fellow marchers and began leading a chant of "stop the cruelty now." As they continued to chant, the religious group began a chant of their own. Caught between the two groups, I silently sidled my way through the crowd and hurried for the door.

Once inside, I headed for the newsroom. As I approached the newsroom door, I could hear the shrill sound of telephones ringing. Opening the door, I stepped inside. I stood and watched for a moment as reporters dashed to and fro to the accompaniment of the ringing telephones. No story I had ever worked on had produced such a reaction.

Walking across the newsroom, I caught sight of Bill Grog, one of the paper's political columnists. "And here's the guy who's responsible for all of this," announced Grog. I looked around as the reporters in the room stopped to stare at me.

"The phones have been ringing off the hook all morning," explained Grog. "I mean, the missing link? An ape that can talk? I know you were looking for an exclusive, but this is hardly the way to go about getting one, Stone."

"But it's all true," I replied. "I saw him myself."

"Well, apparently the police doubt your powers of observation. They issued a denial."

"Just covering their ass. Two officers have already seen him, and one shot him in the arm."

Grog shrugged. "Just telling you what they're saying."

I grimaced, and continued walking toward my city editor's desk. I was met by an angry stare.

"Stone, are you sure that ape talked to you?" he asked. "Because we've been getting calls all morning that it's a scientific impossibility. Meanwhile, there's some scientist who says he has applied for a patent on a creature that is part human and part animal. He says he wants the government to define exactly what a human being is."

"Well, I'm sure that creature is real, although whether he's actually a human being I cannot say," said a voice from behind.

I turned to see Doctor Quant and Sandra standing behind me. "Thank God, you're here, doctor," I said.

"Don't worry, my boy, your story has been a smashing success," he said. "It won't be long before Biocea is forced to pull the plug on Project Dawning."

"But apes can't talk," the city editor continued to argue.

"Ordinary apes can't," Doctor Quant replied, "but this is not an ordinary ape. Besides, recent research has shown that bonobo apes have the ability to learn humanlike communication techniques."

"Yes, doctor, but isn't all just a form of mimicry?"

"I'm afraid not. According to a recent study, bonobos, which are a rare chimpanzee species, have been found to possess language comprehension. Using a keyboard of lexigrams, or symbols, the apes have been taught to communicate as well as a two-and-a-half-year-old child. Indeed, scientists say chimpanzees of all types exhibit some form of culture in their behavior. According to one study, the chimpanzee has a remarkable ability to invent new customs and technologies, such as using sticks to feed on ants, and pass these on socially to other chimpanzees. The research found at least thirty-nine customs related to the chimps' tool use, grooming, and courtship. Now, consider Ngila, whose genes have been manipulated through the use of human DNA. It's not that hard to believe that he developed the ability to talk."

"And what about the religious fanatics who refuse to believe in evolution?"

"Let them transport themselves to another century. The days of blindly following the antiquated notions of the Bible are over. It's quite funny when you think about it. They readily accept the words of a God whose existence has never been proven, and yet, dispute mountains of concrete scientific evidence that clearly demonstrates our evolutionary development. If there's a God, let Him show Himself and explain the evidence Himself."

"Don't quote him on that!" shouted my editor. "The last thing this newspaper needs is to be accused of disputing the existence of God."

"But he's right," I argued.

"Whether he's right or not, we have to find a more diplomatic way of explaining all this to the people."

"Copernicus was probably told the same thing all those centuries ago," said Doctor Quant.

I looked at him and nodded my head. "Well, they'll have to believe it when that creature is finally caught," I said.

"If he's ever caught," corrected my editor. "Right now, the police are denying that such a creature exists. They say they're still looking for a man who they believe is the murderer."

"Then they're denying the facts," I said.

"Maybe, but until that creature is caught, there's no way to prove he exists."

"Well, we know he exists," interjected Sandra. "We've seen him and heard him speak."

"I hope that's enough," said my editor. "For the paper's sake, I hope that's enough."

Chapter Twenty-Five
New York Herald

THE MISSING LINK IS MISSING

By Hudge Stone

The "Monster of Central Park," which is actually a genetically engineered "missing link," is missing.

Known as Ngila, the part human, part gorilla chimera, has been taken by Doctor Luther Steele, head of the Biocea company, to an unknown destination. Some, however, are questioning whether the creature even exists.

But this reporter has seen the creature, and has even talked to him. In exclusive interviews with the *Herald*, inside the Biocea laboratories, both the creature and Doctor Steele told this reporter all about their views on life and why the experiments took place.

As part of those interviews, Doctor Steele explained he brought Ngila to New York City to influence his environment and prompt greater evolutionary changes in the creature.

"We had already done statistical studies that proved environment was extremely important in determining a person's IQ," he said. "Ngila was only familiar with the rain forests of the Congo. I decided he needed a modern environment in order to prompt his intellect to develop to its full potential. And New York City was the perfect place to bring about this development."

Now that the creature is missing, it has been speculated that Doctor Steele has brought him to another location to again prompt new changes in the creature's intellect. Where that would be is not known.

Ngila was created through the use of human DNA in laboratories set up in the African nation of Congo. Before he fully matured, the creature was taken from Africa to New York City by Doctor Steele and the Biocea corporation.

The problem is the creature is a killer like the early ancestors of human beings. While in New York City, he is thought to be responsible for several murders, which include eating the victim's brain. Doctor Steele explained the creature does this to consume needed protein and fat, just as our early ancestors did.

Meanwhile, police said they are searching the New York City area, but have their doubts that anyone will be found. An official police statement doubted the existence of any kind of creature responsible for the multiple murders.

"We will have no further comment until an official investigation is completed," the statement said.

Protesters have been marching outside the *Herald* offices complaining stories about the creature go against long-held religious beliefs and show a cruelty to living things. One of the religious groups called the *Herald* stories "blasphemous."

According to the Reverend James Matthews, leader of the group, "the Bible tells us that God created man from the dust of the earth and that is what we shall always believe. There is no spark of the divine in an ape. That is the providence of man, and of mankind alone."

Another group, protesting the unethical treatment of animals, called the experiments "cruel."

According to both Doctor Steele and Doctor Dekko Quant, who headed the government's human genome study in Washington, creatures such as Ngila can be used for human transplants, test drugs, provide a key to innumerable human illnesses, and even unlock the secrets of the human brain.

That is, of course, if the creature even exists. This reporter and Doctor Quant have been witnesses to the creature's existence, however, and the only question seems to be where Doctor Steele has taken him.

-END-

Chapter Twenty-Six
Hudge Stone

I couldn't help thinking my career was over. It had been days since the missing link story had appeared, and still there was no sign of Doctor Steele or the creature.

Sandra moved close to me, speaking in a low voice. "I'm sure he'll be caught eventually," she said. "I mean, he's pretty easy to spot, don't you think?" She looked at me and smiled.

I couldn't help but frown. "No, you don't understand. He could be back in the jungles of the Congo by now, or in some South American country. All Doctor Steele needed was a plane waiting for him somewhere, and boom, he's gone. My God, he could be anywhere. And where does that leave me? Totally humiliated, and possibly without a job. Some exclusive. Now I'm left starting all over again, back on the night police beat, my reputation utterly ruined."

"It doesn't matter to me, Hudge. I'm in love with you."

"Now I told you not to get involved with me. I'm just some poor schnook beating my brains out for a paycheck. A measly paycheck I obtain by witnessing the nefarious actions of the human race. Oh, yes, a paycheck, by being the first to look at some blood-stained body that was the product of some madman's whim. Or a blazing building with some undernourished child trapped inside. Or people sleeping in a rat infested building because they no longer have the will or mental capabilities to continue the struggle in an uncaring world. And then I have to listen to some cynical cop tell me the rest of the gory details, or some haughty psychologist babble about why it happened. And after all that, I have to go back and write it all up in a nice, succinct bundle of words in as little time as possible, always aware of a deadline that expires every night. You get to the point where you hate everyone, or just don't give a damn anymore. That's what I do for a living. Don't get involved with me, Sandie. You're still beautiful, go find someone who can provide you some happiness."

"But don't you see? I don't care what you do for a living. I don't even care about the monster anymore. All I care about is you. And you're not the only one who's dissatisfied with his job, I can tell you that. What about taking dictation, and typing your fingers to the bone for a measly paycheck? What about listening to every ridiculous thing your boss tells you, as he tries to grope you behind the copying machine? No one has it easy, Hudge. But if two people really care about each other, then maybe, all of that doesn't matter."

"But I can't provide you with everything I would want to give you, Sandie. That's why this story was so important to me. I mean, it could've provided everything. A raise, a promotion, maybe even a book. And then we could've thumbed our noses at the world, and maybe even have obtained some form of happiness. But that's not going to happen, I realize that now."

"I don't care about any of it. We have each other. And maybe starting over isn't such a bad thing, anyway. Besides, there's still a chance that monster will turn up somewhere. I don't believe Doctor Steele fled the country. I mean, somebody would've seen something. And don't forget, Molly is with them. She would've alerted somebody, I'm sure of it."

"Maybe, but until he's found my journalistic career is in serious jeopardy. I mean, everybody thinks I'm on a wild goose chase. And I don't blame them. Even Doctor Quant and the genome papers are being doubted. A Biocea official I talked to today said there were no such experiments taking place at the company. Can you believe it? No such experiments."

"So they're denying it, Hudge. What did you expect them to do? Tell everybody that the missing link is running around? So let them deny it. We know what we saw. I mean, the damned thing kissed me, for heaven's sake."

"The only good idea he ever had." I smiled, and put my arm around Sandra. "You know, maybe you're right," I finally said. "I mean, how far can Doctor Steele get with a caveman and a pregnant woman? And even if they never find him, I guess everything will be all right."

"Now you're talking. It'll all work out, you'll see. And you know you'll always have me."

I looked at her, then bolted to my feet, and jumped up onto the couch. Grunting and snorting, I glared down at her with a tilt of my head. "You, mate," I shouted, pointing at her.

Sandra laughed. "You know you're quite convincing as the missing link," she said.

"I am a man," I grunted, stepping up and down upon the couch.

"I'll be the judge of that," she replied.

I smiled, and slid back down on the couch and into Sandra's arms. I kissed her, and we fell into a passionate embrace.

"Now I hope that was the reason you came over to my apartment," she whispered. "Instead of complaining about some missing monster."

"You know it's the reason. I've loved you ever since I first spotted you in the park talking to that police officer. I felt sorry for Rob, but to me it only meant that you were now free to be mine. And when that creature brought you back to that room, I couldn't control my feelings any longer. I just knew I had to have you. You don't know how scared I was when I saw that creature carry you off into the park. I thought he was going to kill you or something."

"But what if he raped me, Hudge? Would you still love me?"

"More than ever, darling. I love you more than anything else in the world."

We kissed, and then fell once more into a feverish embrace. I felt my heart beating fast, the passion seizing my very being. Sandra then sat up and began unbuttoning her top. She playfully held it up and then let it drop to the floor. I smiled, and took off my shirt. She then stood up, and taking hold of my hand, led me into the bedroom.

Sliding onto the bed, she carefully discarded the rest of her clothing, and watched in anticipation as I did the same. I then slid next to her, and soon our bodies were entwined in rhythmic splendor. The time slowly melted away as we passionately explored each other's bodies, and then, after near exhaustion, I sat up, reached over, and turned on the television.

"I've got to see if they caught the creature," I said.

"No one will ever accuse you of being an incurable romantic," she replied.

Flipping through the channels, I stopped when I came to an anchorwoman in red in the midst of reading the news.

"Police say they will continue the investigation, although there have not been any recent sightings of the creature. Meanwhile, officials have termed the Herald story a hoax, and have called on the paper to issue a retraction."

I looked dejectedly at Sandra and pounded my fist on the bed. "Damn," I said. "Where the hell is that creature, anyway?"

"I told you I'm not a very lucky person," she said. "Everything in my life has always included some kind of disaster causing people to leave me. Why, even my parents divorced when I was ten years old."

I looked at her and turned off the television. "Sandie, don't. All that is in the past. I'm with you now, and no matter what, I'll never leave you. You can count on it."

I leaned over, kissed her, and wrapped my arms around her.

"Oh, Hudge," she moaned. "If only I could believe you."

"Don't worry, nothing can make me leave."

We held each other in the darkness, a darkness disturbed only by the spangled gaze of moonlight peeking through the open window.

"I am here to announce we have created a mosquito that has been genetically modified and will help eradicate malaria," said Doctor Carl Strickland, president of Biocea Systems, as he stared into the bright lights of the television cameras. "This mosquito, which carries an extra gene and produces a green fluorescent protein, will be visible under ultraviolet light and wholly constructed in the laboratory."

"But what about Ngila?" I asked from a crowd of reporters who had been sent to cover the scheduled press conference. "I mean, are you going to tell us what you've done with that creature?"

Doctor Strickland glared at me for a moment, and then noticing the television cameras, began to smile. "I would like to announce that Biocea will no longer perform research of any kind on human beings," he said. "But animal experiments and other basic research will continue. You see, it is the only way to make certain of the effectiveness of our methods and treatments."

"But what about a creature that is part ape and part human?" I shouted. "What does Biocea plan to do about that kind of research?"

Strickland paused for a moment, resting his hands on the lectern, and attempted another grin. "This creature you are referring to, Mr. Stone, is not a part of Biocea's current research plans. I'm sorry you persist in pursuing such questioning and then writing articles without first checking the facts."

"But I've seen him and heard him speak—"

"Really, Mr. Stone, as I said such a creature is not a part of Biocea's current plans, and even if he were, I doubt very much whether even we would be able to create such a being at the present time."

"And I suppose you know nothing about a Doctor Luther Steele."

Doctor Strickland looked at me, and slid his fingers through his graying hair. "Doctor Steele happens to be a respected member of Biocea's staff and is involved with our current project—"

"Then you admit he is involved in genetic engineering experiments."

Strickland grimaced. "Not the experiments you have in mind, Mr. Stone. Why, this whole monster thing is something cooked up by your paper to obviously increase circulation. But, as far as it being reality, that is quite another matter."

"You know nothing about Project Dawning?"

"Let me just say that Project Dawning was an outgrowth of a government study that became too costly and produced less than successful results. The study, however, has led to other advances, including our current experimentation with mosquitoes. You see, substituting genes we were able to cause the malaria-carrying Anopheles mosquito to produce antibodies that destroyed the malaria parasite…"

I slowly sat down, knowing Doctor Strickland had no intention of addressing anything having to do with Ngila or Doctor Steele.

"…We have also had some success in changing the mosquito's behavior so it feeds on animals instead of humans," Doctor Strickland continued. "The transformed green mosquitoes are only the beginning of the development of new approaches for malaria control."

I jotted down Strickland's words, doubting whether Ngila would ever be seen again.

"The transgenic malaria mosquitoes are created after we inject the embryos while they are still soft," Doctor Strickland was saying. "This spreads the resistant gene through the mosquito."

I stood up, and began walking to the door, deciding I would complete this latest story back at the office after making a few telephone calls. It was then I noticed the tall man in the black suit and sunglasses standing in a corner of the room. It was definitely one of the same men who had attacked me inside my apartment and was responsible for murdering Doctor Lido.

I hurried through the door, wondering if I should attempt to confront the man, or find a police officer. I rushed to the other door, and switching on my tape recorder, swung it open, and stepped inside. I glanced toward the corner of the room, anticipating some sort of scuffle, when I noticed the man had vanished.

I surveyed the room, but failed to see any sign of the man. Then I glanced at the lectern, where Doctor Strickland was in the midst of shaking hands with various colleagues. There was a strange glint in his eyes, and I watched as he turned his head, and glared at me. Then, slowly, a smile emerged across his face.

The newsroom chattered with activity, the tension of deadlines soaring through the air. I hurried to my desk attempting to avoid the disapproving glare of my city editor, knowing the monster still had not been located. I knew if the paper was forced to issue a retraction of my story, my career could be ruined. One thing an editor could not tolerate was playing with the facts, or fabricating a story entirely, for they knew it could bring a great newspaper to its knees. The only thing a newspaper had was its integrity and its reputation.

I slumped down in my chair, wanting to hide, wanting to go anywhere but sit there at my desk, out in the open, among the reproving glances of my fellow reporters. I finally stood up, and as quietly as possible, hurried off to the cafeteria. I thought maybe I could hide there for a few minutes, grab a cup of coffee, and hope for the best.

I was headed for the coffee machine, hoping I would go unnoticed, wanting to disappear, when I heard a voice from behind.

"Hey, Stone, have you heard anything more about your monster?"

It was Devlin McCracken, a political reporter, a quiet, unassuming man whose glasses hid the determined look of one who doubted the accepted notions of the general population.

I looked at him, shook my head, wondering if McCracken had decided to support me during these uncertain days. "Not a word," I finally replied. "I've already given up all hope of ever finding him. He could be anywhere in the world by now."

"What about that scientist who had been supplying you with information?"

"He already went back to Washington. He said he would call me if anything turned up. Well, I don't expect to hear anything more from him for quite a while."

"Tough break, but I think it took guts to go with the story in the first place. I hope it all works out."

I smiled. I watched as McCracken walked away, retrieved a cup of coffee from the machine, and decided to head back to the newsroom, feeling renewed hope surging through my body. In time, everything would return to normal, I assured myself, the monster story becoming a fleeting memory in the onrush of daily events. The only good thing that would come out of it, as far as I was concerned, was my relationship with Sandra.

I hurried across the newsroom, glanced at the clock, and sat back down at my desk. Feeling a little tired, I hoped the day would quickly fade into the past. I then placed my coffee down, and reached for the phone, when it suddenly began to ring.

"Stone here."

"Yes, Mr. Stone, I think it's time we meet once again," said the voice on the other end.

The voice sounded familiar, but I couldn't remember where I had heard it before. "I'm sorry, but I'm really not sure who this is," I said, hoping I hadn't discouraged the caller.

"Oh, geez, Stone, it's Steele. Doctor Steele."

The name echoed through my brain, causing me to bolt to attention. A wave of adrenaline suddenly surged through my body, which had been in the throes of listlessness all day.

"Doctor Steele?" I repeated incredulously. "Where are you?"

"About two hours from the city, Stone. It's an easy drive."

I exhaled, the sweat forming on my forehead. Not only had Doctor Steele reemerged, but he was still only a few miles from the city.

"Well, I'd like to come up there and talk to you," I said, trying to stay as calm as possible.

"Exactly what I had in mind. There's a lot I have to say, and I think you should be the one I talk to before I introduce Ngila to the world. You see, we're almost ready, Stone."

"You mean the experiments have been completed?"

"Well, I don't think they'll ever be totally completed because, you see, Ngila is still changing. But I do think he has progressed enough to finally allow my scientific colleagues a chance to examine him. I plan on doing this sometime soon. In the meantime, I thought you'd come out here and take a look around. A sort of preliminary introduction, if you will."

I paused for a moment. I could feel my heart pumping, awakening my body from a prolonged stupor. "I think that's a good idea," I finally said. "I could be there later today."

"I was hoping you'd say that. You'll be very surprised at the changes Ngila has undergone since you last saw him. There's only one condition, Stone. I want you to come alone and not tell anyone where you're going. No police, Stone. And, oh yes, this is something I have no desire for Quant to be involved in. Do you understand?"

"That shouldn't be a problem. He already went back to

Washington."

"Sounds like Quant. Never did complete anything he started. Well, then, Mr. Stone, I'll look forward to seeing you. You'll enjoy the ride. Very scenic. Anyway, it's about time you got away from that nasty city. You need to breathe in some fresh suburban air. It's already done wonders for Ngila, that's for sure."

"I'll do my best to get there as soon as possible, doctor."

"Very good, Stone. And remember, come alone and don't tell anyone where you're going."

"But what about my editor?"

"Tell him something very important has come up. That you need a few hours, and when you come back, you'll tell him all about it. Tell him you'll bring back a story that will be well worth the time spent away from the office. But I warn you, Stone, whatever you do, don't tell him the truth. There are very few people I can trust at this point in time and you, my friend, happen to be one of them. You realize, of course, if anything does go wrong, it could lead to a lot of needless bloodshed. I'm talking about Molly, and possibly, even Sandra. You wouldn't want that to happen, would you, Stone?"

"Sandie? What have you done to Sandie?"

"Relax, Mr. Stone, I'm just trying to explain to you the possible consequences for any imprudent actions you may take. As long as you follow my instructions, everything will be all right. Do you understand?"

"I'm quite willing to come alone, Doctor Steele, but I don't like being threatened. No matter how good the story might be. Now let's get this straight, you harm one hair of either of those ladies and I'll have every officer in the state come down on you so hard you won't know what hit you. Do *you* understand?"

"Now, now, Mr. Stone, I didn't intend for us to argue. I have no intention of harming either lady, please be assured. I just wanted to make sure you didn't do anything foolhardy, that's all."

I thought for a moment. "You can be quite sure I'll come alone, doctor," I finally said.

"Good, then I'll be waiting for you." I heard the click of the phone, and I hung up. My euphoria over the story had changed to deep concern.

I hadn't been prepared for Doctor Steele to threaten people I cared for. Especially Sandie. I began to worry whether something had happened to her, and decided to call. I was prepared to tell her everything, no matter what Doctor Steele had said.

Picking up the phone, I dialed her office number. I waited for it to ring, and then heard a voice on the other end. It was Sandie, and she sounded as if nothing at all had happened. Apparently, however, she detected some concern in my voice.

"Hudge? Is everything all right?"

"It is now, my darling. I thought something might have happened to you."

"Why would you think that, Hudge? Is something going on I should know about?"

I wondered whether I should tell her about Doctor Steele. Why worry her? Then I decided someone should know where I was in case something went wrong.

"I just received a call from an old friend of ours," I began. "Doctor Steele."

"Doctor Steele?" she repeated. "Where is he?"

"Hiding in a house in the suburbs. I'm getting ready to leave right now."

"Oh, Hudge, do you think it's safe to go there alone? I mean, Ngila will be there. Do you think it's worth it?"

"I have to go, Sandie. It's a story that may not ever come my way again. I know it might be dangerous, but that's why I wanted to call you and let you know where I was. In case, something did happen."

"You're going alone?"

"Those were the terms of the agreement. It's just that, well, he made threats if I decided to tell anyone. I just had to know if you were all right."

"Threats against me, Hudge?"

"He mentioned you and Molly. I just needed to make sure nothing had happened to you. No story is worth that."

"I'll be all right, Hudge. You just make sure you get Molly out of there. If I don't hear from you by tonight, I'm calling the police."

"Please, Sandie, no police. I already promised Doctor Steele, and I want this story very badly. It could help restore my reputation, as well as leading to all those things we talked about. Do I have your word?"

"As long as you promise me that you'll call tonight," she said. "I want to make sure you're coming back, Hudge. I don't want to lose anyone else to this whole Project Dawning thing."

"You can count on it. I'll interview Doctor Steele, and then call you on my cell phone."

"Okay, Hudge, but if I don't hear from you, I'm going to tell the police everything. Doctor Steele should be arrested, anyway. As far as Ngila is concerned, I think he should be shipped back to the Congo or placed in a cage."

"But he's almost a man, Sandie."

"A murderer, you mean. And what about Molly? She's already been raped, and who knows what they've done to her since."

"It'll all be over very soon, darling. Anyway, I have to get going. I'll speak to you tonight."

"Okay, Hudge, but you take care of yourself. Remember, I'm still in love with you."

I smiled. I pledged my love to her, and then, after a repeated good-bye, I hung up. I now had to decide whether to tell my city editor. Walking over to his desk, I attempted to explain why I needed the night off. When my editor refused, I decided to tell him about Doctor Steele.

"You're kidding," my editor replied. "He called you after making you sweat it out for so long?"

"Yes, but he told me not to tell anyone, not even you."

"Nonsense. Now you take a company car, and get out there right away. And, this time, Stone, take a photographer with you. No matter what happens, I, at least, want a photograph of that creature. No one's going to accuse this paper of fabricating a story. This time, I want some concrete evidence."

"I can't. I gave him my word that I would come alone."

"All right, then have one of them give you a camera. You can hide it underneath your jacket or something. I don't care what you do, but I want a photograph of that damned beast. This paper's reputation and your continued employment, I might add, depends upon it, Stone."

I nodded, hurried across the newsroom, and after some searching, located a camera. Several minutes later, I was in a car and on my way to Doctor Steele.

Chapter Twenty-Seven
The Human Genome

A printed manuscript of the human genome would require a stack of paper higher than the Washington Monument. It can be thought of as an immense encyclopedia written in a single enormous sentence of 3.1 billion letters, with virtually no punctuation included. A copy of this long, rambling molecular sentence is found inside almost every one of the body's one hundred trillion cells.

The text consists of individual genes, ranging in size from about one thousand to one hundred thousand letters. The letters are actually one of the four chemical bases that constitute the double-helix DNA spiral. The order of those bases provide a certain set of instructions that regulates how a cell carries out essential tasks, such as producing hormones and reproducing itself.

Even after all the letters of the encyclopedia have been identified, scientists must still attempt to convert the mass of coded letters into readable text. The problem is much of the book includes stretches of text known as junk DNA, which may not be junk at all, causing scientists to have to try to identify the meaningful portions with the help of computers. Much of the work is accomplished through comparative studies with other animals, such as the mouse. But this is a slow process, utilizing supercomputers analyzing data seven days a week, twenty-four hours a day, or millions of times the computing power it took to land a man on the moon. And it all just began in the twentieth century, although scientists agreed that they would discover the function of most of the genes sometime during the twenty-first century. Indeed, scientists were confident they would uncover most of the genes involved in such illnesses as heart disease, diabetes, asthma, and manic depression, even if those illnesses were influenced by multiple genes and environmental factors.

Chapter Twenty-Eight
Hudge Stone

I looked up and realized it would soon be dark, the sun steadily falling toward the horizon, an orange flare streaking the sky. I had been traveling along the highway for hours, still searching for a sign that would lead me to the residence of Doctor Steele. I was worried I was somehow lost, and would never find the house once darkness descended upon the landscape. Deciding whether to turn back, I suddenly caught sight of a large green sign in the distance. Stepping on the accelerator, the sign moved swiftly toward me until I could finally make out the words. OXFORD LAKE, ONE MILE.

I let out a jubilant shout. I pressed down on the accelerator, and was soon rolling down the exit ramp. A few moments later, I was headed down a narrow roadway, a row of verdant hills towering in the distance. Doctor Steele had told me to stay on the roadway until I reached the foot of the hills.

The sun, meanwhile, had slipped below the horizon, leaving behind a crimson trail amid the dark blue sky. When I had reached the end of the roadway, I glanced to my right and noticed an old, white clapboard house somewhat obscured by a clump of trees. Gliding down the long driveway, I came to a halt as I neared the front walkway.

I slid out of the car and made my way to the front door, looking up at the windows and noticing they were devoid of light. Knocking on the door several times, I soon heard someone stirring inside. After a moment, the door opened, and standing among the shadows was Doctor Steele.

"Come in, Mr. Stone," he said. "I trust you are alone."

I nodded, and stepped inside. The house was enshrouded in darkness, a single light glowing in a nearby hallway. I looked around, hoping I would see or hear Molly somewhere inside.

"There is no one here, Mr. Stone, except for Ngila and myself," said Doctor Steele, seemingly aware of my intentions. "All of my work is being done in the basement. Would you like a drink?"

I shook my head, and followed Doctor Steele to the living room. "Is Biocea aware that you're here?" I finally asked.

"Yes, Mr. Stone, they wanted me to take Ngila away from the city to give people time to forget. It is quite a change of pace from all the noise of New York City, don't you agree? A person can easily get used to such a life."

"Doctor Strickland denied there even was a Ngila or a Project Dawning."

"Quite understandable," replied Doctor Steele. "We really must be careful, Mr. Stone, as to who knows about our little study. You see, there is quite a lot of money at stake."

"But then, why are you prepared to tell me?"

"Because, you see, Mr. Stone, the experiment is almost completed and I thought it was time for the people to know something about what we had accomplished. I am quite sure once they know about Ngila and his most astonishing capabilities they will have no choice but to admit that it was all very much worthwhile. I mean, think of the benefits to the entire human race our experiment will provide."

"Even if it meant the deaths of a few innocent people..."

"Exactly, Mr. Stone. Once the people know the details of our study, they will have to agree it was well worth the price of a few lives. No one could have imagined the overwhelming success we would obtain when Project Dawning began, but now it is incontestable. We didn't even know what we would find when we organized that first expedition of local tribesmen, and then with shotguns and tranquilizer darts, headed for the Congo rain forest. We had heard reports of the animals behaving strangely in one part of the jungle. No one knew why, although the Shinkolobwe mine, which had been used since the 1940s for the mining of uranium and had been used to produce the first atomic bombs, was located in that very area."

"The area had been contaminated by radiation?"

"Yes, Mr. Stone, the Geiger counter was constantly chattering. We knew we needed to find the specimen we originally released into the wild to confirm our worst fears. It wasn't long before I heard the tribesmen shouting in the distance, alerting me to an animal weaving his way through the dense undergrowth. I was a few yards behind, and immediately ran through the lush vegetation hoping to catch up. I had given them specific orders not to kill any of the animals they might find, but as I rushed toward the shouting, I was still worried one of them might decide to deal the poor beast a fatal blow and ruin any opportunity of bringing it back alive."

Doctor Steele paused for a moment, dabbed his forehead with a handkerchief, and continued. "As I got closer, the tribesmen fell silent. I could see them standing in front of a clump of ferns waving their arms excitedly, pointing at some bushes. When they caught sight of me, they began whispering the alert once again. We waited for a few moments, until there was a low murmuring followed by a high-pitched shrieking. It echoed through the jungle, and I knew it meant he was getting ready to attack. Sure enough, the ferns parted, and a snarling ape charged toward us. The men gasped at the sight of him, and began running in the other direction. The ape, however, succeeded in grabbing one of the men, and holding his throat, unsheathed his teeth, and bit into his neck. Blood gushed from the wound as the man slumped forward, and let out a piercing groan."

"He was killed?" I asked.

"Sure enough," replied Doctor Steele. "We watched as he fell to the ground, and then one of the men raised his shotgun and fired at the attacking ape. The creature jerked to a halt, and crumpled to the ground. I then bent down and examined the tribesman, but he was already dead.

"We then gathered around the motionless ape and were very much surprised by what we saw. First of all, the protruding canine teeth in his open mouth were spatulate, not conical, as is usually found in apes. The rest of his face also contained many elements that combined made the beast appear somewhat human. I was especially fascinated by the way the skull rounded back above the creature's eyes, producing a kind of human forehead. This is, of course, unheard of in gorillas, the skull usually winding back almost horizontally. We also noticed the creature's body was devoid of the usual dense hair covering. Surely, something serious had befallen him. I checked the Geiger counter again and saw that it was clicking wildly.

"I wanted the chance to study the specimen further, and ordered the beast be brought back to our compound. There was no telling what effect the heavy radiation had had on his body, but I was eager to attempt to find out. The tribesmen carried the body to a cage we had brought along, and then chattering noisily amongst themselves, they retrieved their fellow tribesman's body and we started back through the jungle.

"I was curious as to what the tribesmen had been talking about amongst themselves so I asked my African assistant and interpreter. He turned toward me with a solemn look in his eyes, as if he were frightened by the mere mention of the words, and then, with some hesitation, finally replied.

"'Gorilla ghost,' he said."

Doctor Steele sipped at his drink, and smiled. After a pronounced pause, he continued. "We had gone only a few feet when we heard another noise from behind the ferns. I looked at the tribesmen, and motioned to them to prepare for another attack. Placing down the cage containing the dead gorilla, they reached for their shotguns. The blood-soaked body of the murdered tribesman was also placed on the ground as we listened for additional movement among the bushes, hoping to locate the source of the sounds. After a few moments, we could hear a soft moaning, which sounded as if it were emanating from the mouth of a child. Slowly approaching the ferns, I carefully pulled back the branches. There, sitting on the ground and still softly moaning, was a young gorilla.

"I was overwhelmed by the sight of the small figure, and stood staring at him until finally deciding to approach. As I moved closer, however, he looked up and sneered, discharging a sort of hissing sound.

"I tried talking to the young creature, hoping the sound of my voice and the reassuring movements of my hands would help calm him.

Rising to his feet, he bent over, his arms dangling in front of him, and dashed toward the clearing. He halted at the sight of the tribesmen aiming their weapons in his direction. I hurried after him, imploring the men not to shoot. The tribesmen stared at the young ape and, lowering their guns, began to laugh. But the young creature ignored them, instead turning his attention to the motionless body of the dead ape. He smiled at the air, darted backwards, and began to scream. The men were amused by these actions, and began to laugh once again."

I suddenly interrupted. "This young gorilla, was it Ngila?"

"Let me finish, Mr. Stone," replied Doctor Steele. "You'll get your answer soon enough."

I fell silent, intently listening to Doctor Steele as he began speaking once more.

"This young gorilla suddenly stood before us beating his chest. Then, reaching down, he grabbed a handful of vegetation and began throwing it at the men. You understand, some gorillas are prone to such actions before they attack. But watching this young ape attempting to intimidate them caused the men to burst into laughter.

"*Ngila,*' laughed the tribesmen. That's the Mbeti word for gorilla, Mr. Stone. *Ngila.*"

"Yes, Doctor Quant told me the same thing."

"Well, anyway, I watched the young ape's actions, and stepping forward, hoped to convey our good intentions. I smiled at him and then lifted my hand in a gesture of peace. He looked at me and charged forward. Holding my arms out to embrace him, he opened his mouth, and bit down on one of my fingers. As I let out a cry of pain, the tribesmen watched with delight.

"I looked at them, and laughing, bent down and lifted him into the air. He struggled in my arms, angrily grunting his objection, but eventually calmed down and accepted us as new friends. We decided to name him, Ngila, and take him back with us to the compound.

"I was so excited with finding him, I told the tribesmen to leave the dead ape behind. I then grabbed his hand and began walking back toward the clearing where a truck waited in the tall savanna grass. We had walked only a few steps when he pulled his hand away, and dashed back toward the fallen ape. He stood staring at the lifeless body, grunting nervously, and then, raising his head, began to scream.

"I approached him and gently placed my hands on his shoulders in an attempt to comfort him, but he turned and hissed, wriggled from my grasp, and began to scream once again. I realized he would not let us leave the dead ape behind, and so, I motioned for the tribesmen to place the ape back in the cage. Ngila eagerly watched as the men picked up the ape's body, and placing him inside the cage, lifted it and carried it away. I watched as Ngila stood alone for a moment, made some sort of hooting sound, and then ran after the men. He followed the cage all the way back to the clearing, every so often looking back at me, and grunting his approval."

Doctor Steele took another sip of his drink, paused for a moment, and then frowned. "Well, we found out later that dead ape was apparently Ngila's father," he said. "He had been quite damaged by the radiation, although it seems Ngila was somehow not severely affected. Ngila, of course, turned out to be one of our test subjects that we released into the wild. It was miraculous that we found him again." He paused once again. "And now, Mr. Stone, do you understand how special Ngila is? Why, even before we knew who he was, it turned out he had developed a distinct and most delightful personality. The experiments only emphasized this natural possession."

"Then why make him a killer?"

"It was only a preliminary side effect, Mr. Stone. You see, Ngila is changing all the time. Why, he's become much more peaceful since you last saw him."

"I wish I could believe you, doctor."

"But you must, that's why I had you come. You don't have to take my word for it, Mr. Stone. I will show you."

Doctor Steele arose and then began walking toward a basement door, motioning me to follow him.

"This, Mr. Stone, is my laboratory," Doctor Steele said, opening the white basement door. "It is quite modern, I assure you. A sort of home away from home, if you will."

I peered inside. I was amazed at the amount of modern equipment lining the stark white walls.

As we made our way down the wooden staircase, I noticed Ngila standing in one of the corners of the room. Somehow his features seemed more refined, as if his entire body was still undergoing the rigors of evolution. He was still half-bent, with huge rolling shoulders, but his face appeared more genteel, the eyebrow-ridges, broad nose, and flat forehead softened by both time and the rearrangement of his genes.

"You remember Mr. Stone," said Doctor Steele, upon entering the room. "He's here to do a story on us before I introduce you to the world at large."

Ngila grunted, glaring at us in what seemed to be a rather hostile manner. "Don't want world," he said in a throaty whisper. "Want to go back to jungle."

Despite his appearance, it was quite apparent Ngila's brain had not evolved as rapidly as his body. Listening to his words and the inflection in his voice, one would say his intelligence was still equal to that of a child, yet, in spirit and in the world of science and experimentation, he was equal to a human ancestor millions of years old.

"There is nothing for you back in the jungle, my friend," replied Doctor Steele. "You represent the beginning, the struggle against Nature, while all around are the fruits of that victory. It would not serve any purpose for you to go back to where you no longer belong."

As I looked at Ngila, I remembered that I had forgotten my camera back in the car. "Would you mind, doctor, if I took a photograph of Ngila?" I asked. "It would be very helpful in attempting to humanize him in the eyes of our readers."

"Go right ahead, Mr. Stone," replied Doctor Steele. "I think it's a perfectly splendid idea."

I hurried back up the wooden staircase, and retrieved the camera from the car. When I returned, Ngila was slumped over, his hands pressed against the side of his head.

"Quite incredible," murmured Doctor Steele. "You see, Mr. Stone, evolution is still taking place. The experiments remain valid."

Ngila groaned, then raised his head and snarled. "Why do this to me? Have felt changes before. Changes hurt Ngila very much. Still they say he is not a man."

"Don't worry, my friend, you'll be all right," replied Doctor Steele. "And soon you'll have evolved into more of a man than you are now — a better man with less violent tendencies."

"Ngila don't want to be man anymore. Want to go back to jungle and live among trees again. Ngila belongs in jungle."

"I'm sorry, my friend, but there is nothing I can do. The experiments are well past the point of no return."

Ngila snarled once again. "You are not Ngila's friend. You care only about changing his body. Doctor have no right to change Ngila. Was happy in jungle."

Doctor Steele frowned, and turned toward me. "He is like Adam who has realized he has lost Eden," he said. "And yet, it is only a memory enhanced by the passing of time."

"But look what you've done to him," I said. "He only wants to be free again."

Doctor Steele dismissed the remark with a wave of his hand. "It is not possible," he said. "Ngila belongs here, helping the human race. Besides, he would no longer be accepted in the jungle. He is more human than animal by now. He must remain. He no longer has any choice."

"Some would say since you have altered his brain, and now that he is more human than animal, he should have a choice. That, by virtue of his place among humankind, he should be able to decide whether he wants his body experimented on any longer. That you don't have the right to keep him against his will."

"And allow him to go back to the jungle? Ridiculous, Mr. Stone. Ngila has a very great purpose on this earth, and I will see that he carries it out. Why, we could learn more about ourselves from studying him than we could from years of conventional research. He is our past, and will help illuminate our future. There are great changes ahead, and Ngila is only the beginning. Why, once we understand DNA, it won't be long before doctors are able to prepare an entire health profile for every individual just by taking a swab of our cheek or skin cells. An entire diet, which will include preventive medicines, will be genetically engineered and prescribed to the patient eliminating disease of every kind. That is what Ngila is a part of, Mr. Stone."

"And what about Ngila?"

"In time, he will get used to living in human civilization. In fact,

Mr. Stone, I plan to keep him here until he finally develops an aversion to chaos and violence. Only until I am satisfied that some behavioral change has, indeed, occurred, would I consider bringing him back to Africa. Then, Mr. Stone, I should think a brand new society of missing links will be created, with Ngila as their leader, showing us how our own society began and what mistakes we made along the way. That surely would be the culmination of Project Dawning."

"And what about all the killing, doctor?"

"A minor matter, Mr. Stone, necessary for the advancement of the human race. Those people gave their lives in the interests of science, a science that will finally include an understanding of the brain through viable research and real time scanning machines. In time, we will be able to change human behavior for the better, as I have changed Ngila's. And this understanding will only lead to even more advances, such as brain implants to aid learning and eliminate mental illness."

"But the people who gave their lives had no say in the matter," I argued.

"Then blame it on the laws of Nature, survival of the fittest," replied Doctor Steele. "That is the only law Ngila obeys."

Upon hearing the words, Ngila stepped forward, his thin lips curled into a frown. "I am only animal to you," he said.

"You are wrong, my friend," replied Doctor Steele. "Maybe at one time I did feel that way, but not at this point. You are an extraordinary creature, my friend. There is so much we need to learn from you. You are everything man had once been — a vicious savage who cared only about his own survival."

"But you said he was more human than animal," I said.

"And so he is, Mr. Stone. Why, look at his face, his hands…why, listen to him speak! Yes, he is a man. Why, Ngila is even on the verge of fashioning tools. Tools, Mr. Stone. The work of early man. And fire? That is no longer one of his fears. In fact, he is on the verge of utilizing it, just as our ancestors did all those centuries ago."

Doctor Steele then reached down and grabbed a Bunsen burner sitting on one of the tables. He lit the flame and pointed it at Ngila, who calmly stared back at it.

"You see, Mr. Stone, not a word of protest or fear." A broad grin spread across Doctor Steele's face as he held the burner in the air, the yellow flame hissing in the light. "Yes, a man. A man who has hurdled the gap between human and beast. A man who can help change the direction of human history. A man."

Upon hearing the words, Ngila growled. "Don't want to be man," he snarled. He then lunged toward one of the laboratory tables and knocked a collection of test tubes to the floor. I turned away when I saw the chemicals inside the tubes splash across the room. When I turned back around, Doctor Steele staggered forward and let out a wrenching scream. Somehow one of the chemicals had spilled upon his clothing and had ignited into flames. The flames flared into the air, engulfing his body, and causing him to step backward. Then he fell to the floor, writhing amid the shattered glass and spattered chemicals.

I took a few steps forward, wanting to help Doctor Steele extinguish the flames, when the spilled chemicals suddenly caught fire and shot across the laboratory. The entire room was soon engulfed in the spreading blaze.

"We'd better get out of here!" I shouted, still attempting to get close to Doctor Steele. I looked for Ngila, but a flame shot up and sizzled across the ceiling.

Fearing for my own life, I rushed up the staircase and out the front door. I stood in the front yard and watched as the flames quickly spread throughout the house. They hissed and crackled, finally spewing out the windows in a brilliant flare of light, and then snarled amid the darkness.

Chapter Twenty-Nine
Hudge Stone

As I stared at the ravaging flames, I heard a tremendous crash toward the rear of the house. Deciding to investigate, I hurried across the grass and noticed the basement window had been shattered. A black figure dashed toward a clump of trees in the distance.

I rushed into the darkness, following the figure, and finally reached the trees. Searching among the shadows, I could hear a deep groaning nearby. As I was about to step forward, something grabbed me from behind.

"No scream," said the voice.

I turned around, and stared into Ngila's fierce eyes. I suppressed an overwhelming urge to shout, and then noticed blood oozing from the creature's shoulder. The rest of his torso had been badly burned.

"You're injured," I finally said.

"Ngila not hurt bad," the hulking figure replied. "But must find place to hide."

"But you're free now to go wherever you like," I said. "Doctor Steele is dead, thereby putting an end to Project Dawning."

"Yes, free," repeated Ngila.

"Perhaps, you'll go back to the jungle."

"Yes, live in jungle."

I could see that Ngila was badly injured, but I tried to ignore it. Instead, I attempted to comfort him with thoughts of his childhood jungle home. Whatever my opinion of the creature's murderous tendencies, I felt he had already been through enough as a victim of the Project Dawning experiments.

"What will you do in the jungle?" I asked.

"Live among the trees," Ngila replied. "Live free."

I watched as Ngila took a step and stumbled forward. He was losing his strength, a strength that had safeguarded his survival in both the jungle and civilization.

"Must hide," he finally said. "People will be coming."

He glanced toward the rolling hills above with an approving grunt. "Will go up there. People will not follow Ngila there."

"But, eventually, they'll come after you, you realize that."

"Will hide among trees. People will not find Ngila."

I watched as the hulking figure attempted to take a few steps toward his stated goal. His legs were unsteady, and finally, he halted with a soft groan emanating from his lips.

"Do you think you can make it, Ngila?" I asked. I knew just by looking at the ailing creature that his attempt up the steep slope was doomed to failure. But Ngila was undaunted by his initial steps, and had only halted in an attempt to regain some of his lost strength.

"Doctor did this to me," he suddenly snarled. "Changed Ngila's body, took him from jungle."

"But didn't he care for you?" I asked. "Didn't he help you become a man?"

Ngila looked at me and growled. "Doctor hurt Ngila. Took him from jungle, beat him, changed his body. Ngila glad doctor no longer lives. Ngila free now. Not meant to live with humans."

Listening to Ngila's words, I realized just how cruel the experiments had been. It was made even worse by the fact that Ngila now knew what had happened to him. He wasn't some ordinary laboratory animal to be experimented on and then disposed of. Ngila now possessed reason, a conscious awareness of the world around him. He was no longer man's possession, but an individual, a member of the human world that had so callously created him.

"Well, I guess you can go where you want," I said.

Without looking back, the hulking figure trudged forward. I watched as he slowly made his way to the foot of the hill. He stopped for a moment, seemed to slump forward, and then continued onward. I could hear sirens moaning in the distance. The fire engines would soon arrive, and with them, people who wouldn't think twice about taking away Ngila's freedom. I peered into the darkness and watched as the figure steadily made his way up the hillside. I found myself hoping Ngila would make it to the summit, and then disappear into the landscape. Maybe he would even find his way back to his beloved jungle. Somehow I believed human beings owed him that much.

I gazed at the darkened figure as he struggled up the hillside. He had almost made it halfway when suddenly his legs trembled and he collapsed to the ground. Dashing through the darkness, I hurried up the slope until I reached the fallen figure. Ngila groaned as I reached down and rolled him onto his back.

"You'll be all right, Ngila," I said. "I'll take you back and we'll care for you. You'll see. We'll make sure you get back to that jungle of yours. Why, I'll take you back there myself."

Ngila looked up at me with a strange look in his eyes. "Free," he murmured.

Then I watched as the creature closed his eyes and the awesome power contained in the massive body seemed to suddenly evaporate. It was as if Ngila had decided to surrender, decided his dream of reaching the jungle was hopelessly out of reach, and that the only freedom he would ever really find was in Death itself. I stared down at the imposing body, realizing Ngila's struggle against both man and Nature was finally over. He was now truly free, his years of torment having finally come to an end. He was now once again a part of Nature, and whether he was man or beast no longer mattered.

I stood up, a great sadness enveloping me, and walked back toward the house. I decided I would leave the body where it was, and wait for someone to discover it in the morning light. At least, Ngila would have a momentary rest amid the darkness. I knew what would happen once they found him. More than likely, he would be studied and dissected in the interests of science.

Walking back through the darkness, I could still see tiny flames flickering in the windows of the house. Firefighters rushed across the lawn pulling long hoses that sent torrents of water gushing against the charred structure. It would be hours before I would be able to head back to the city. I would first have to speak with those in charge, explain to them what had occurred, and then wait for them to retrieve Doctor Steele's body. The story of Ngila would soon be lost among the ardent denials and lack of evidence. It would become just another secret guarded by those in charge in an effort to obfuscate the truth and protect themselves from the protests of an outraged American public.

When they finally asked me what had happened to the creature, I decided I would try to protect Ngila and say he had perished in the flames along with Doctor Steele. I knew, however, that would not be the end of it, for they were bound to discover Ngila's withered body lying on the hillside the next day. But I decided I didn't want to be part of any protracted investigation. I wanted time to think and return to the newspaper, where I would write my story. It would contain the details of Doctor Steele's death, but only a vague reference to Ngila. I wanted to make sure no one would accuse me of imagining some sort of monster ever again. This time, the story of the missing link would be buried amid quotes from Doctor Steele and a discussion of Project Dawning. It would take time before the American public was ready for the truth.

I made my way across the front lawn, the house still heaving smoke into the warm night air. I retrieved my cell phone from my car and decided to call Sandra.

"Hello, darling, I'm coming home," I murmured. I paused for a moment. "Yes, I'm quite fine, but Doctor Steele and Ngila are dead."

I listened to her frantic questions, and tried to remain calm. "It was a fire, Sandie," I said. "I'll tell you all about it when I get back. No, no, I don't know where Molly is. There was no one else in the house except for Doctor Steele and Ngila. We'll just have to keep searching. Maybe the police will find her as part of their investigation."

I listened to the sound of her voice and smiled. "I love you too," I finally replied. "I'll be back very soon and tell you everything that has happened."

As I hung up, I slid back into the front seat of my car and realized something was missing. After a few moments, I finally remembered I had left my camera in Doctor Steele's basement laboratory. The photographs of Ngila, the Monster of Central Park, had been reduced to smoldering ashes.

Chapter Thirty
New York Herald

THE MONSTER OF CENTRAL PARK DIES IN FIRE

By Hudge Stone

Ngila, the Monster of Central Park and the scientifically created Missing Link, died in a fire yesterday in a New York suburban house where he was being prepared by a Doctor Luther Steele to be introduced to the world.

Doctor Steele also died in the blaze.

This reporter, who was granted a personal preview of the monster at the Oxford Lake house, witnessed both deaths before escaping the flames.

It is not known whether the deaths will put an end to the Project Dawning study seeking to create chimeras, or half human and half animal creatures, which Doctor Steele and other scientists have defended as an invaluable source of biological and social information that could help the human race learn more about its past and assist it in the future.

In a wide-ranging exclusive interview with the *Herald* before he died, Doctor Steele explained that Ngila would be shipped back to Africa after extensive study. "Then, I should think a brand new society of missing links will be created, with Ngila as their leader, showing us how our own society began and what mistakes we made along the way," he said.

According to Doctor Steele, Ngila, also known as "The Monster of Central Park" and responsible for several murders in New York City, was the equivalent of the missing link, the legendary transitional creature between humans and apes, as a result of the experiments.

Doctor Steele was so sure Ngila was still evolving into a human being, he attempted to demonstrate to this reporter Ngila's lack of fear of fire. The creature, however, showing a repugnance for being turned into a human being, knocked some chemicals towards a lit Bunsen burner and ignited the fatal fire.

Ultimately, Ngila's story is a sad one, an unwilling victim of scientific experimentation. Because of the experiments, he was turned into a rampaging killer, much like our early human ancestors.

But at the end, Ngila had become aware of his cruel plight. "Doctor hurt Ngila," he told this reporter before dying. "Took him from jungle, beat him, changed his body. Ngila free now. Not meant to live with humans."

Many would agree the Project Dawning experiments were a cruel manipulation of the laws of Nature. Through the use of human DNA, genes — including the one which allows humans to talk — were manipulated, spliced, and transplanted into Ngila's gorilla body.

It was planned that creatures such as Ngila, known as parahumans, would then be used for human transplants, test new drugs, teach us about the workings of the human brain, and undertake dangerous and demeaning work, according to Doctor Steele. He explained that with the cooperation of Biocea Systems he intended to create a whole new race of parahumans, many along the human evolutionary scale.

"In this very building (the Biocea Systems building), we are in the process of creating many Ngilas, utilizing human embryo cells, all in various stages of evolutionary development," he told the *Herald*. "Cro-Magnons, Neanderthals, *Homo erectus*, Australopithecines, all with the manipulation of both human and anthropoid genes."

The creatures would then be taken to various environments, such as New York City, to strengthen their intellect and bring about further evolutionary changes, he said.

Ngila, who Doctor Steele explained was one of his most promising subjects, was taken to New York, which prompted his intellectual development but also turned him into a savage murderer. His brutal killings were punctuated by the eating of the victims' brains.

The Project Dawning study was initially a part of the Human Genome Project, an international research program funded in the United States by the National Institutes of Health and the Department of Energy in Washington, D.C. The $3 billion project eventually uncovered the sequence or exact order of the estimated 20,000 to 25,000 genes in the human body.

Doctor Dekko Quant, a director of the project who personally witnessed Ngila along with this reporter, said that while he was opposed to the methods of the Project Dawning study, its success was undeniable. "Taking into consideration the scientific advances we've made in the past few years, I think the success of the experiment is not that surprising," he told the *Herald*. "It will surely be proven that the greatest discovery of the twentieth century was the structure of DNA."

He stressed the scientific improvements will bring enormous changes in the future. "With our understanding of genes, anything is possible," he said.

-END-

Chapter Thirty-One
Hudge Stone

"I'll come right over, Sandie, just as soon as I finish this story I'm working on." I blew a kiss into the phone, and then placed it back down on my desk. Months had passed since I had returned from the charred ruins of Doctor Steele's house, months that had been filled with some of the happiest days of my life. It was now winter, the threshold of a new year, and I couldn't help but think of the wondrous year that had gone by so swiftly.

After Ngila's body had been found, and people began questioning who the strange creature was, I had written a series of articles detailing the Project Dawning experiments. The stories had subsequently been picked up by the wire services and had been printed across the country. Many of my colleagues expected me to have a chance to win the Pulitzer Prize, while my editors had informed me I would be appointed assistant city editor and be given the raise I had so desperately hoped for. Doctor Quant had later called to tell me that Biocea had announced it had officially abandoned the Project Dawning study.

I realized these events would have made the year special under normal circumstances, but something more important had intervened. My days spent with Sandra had given me a renewed outlook on life. She was everything I had hoped for, and our relationship blossomed into one of mutual respect. I had eventually asked her to marry me, a wedding finally being planned for the spring.

Despite this period of extended happiness, I occasionally thought about Ngila, which invariably caused me to wonder how far man had really come from his anthropoid origins. Was he still not the vicious killer driven by lust and a selfish need to oppress his fellow man? In the midst of pondering these notions, I recalled Doctor Steele's fiery words — the monster is us. It was a statement I came to believe was not as impetuous as it initially seemed.

Meanwhile, the study of the human genome continued. Researchers had recently concluded that more than one-quarter of three major types of cancer were caused by one's genes, although they doubted whether discovering the human genetic code would lead to a total elimination of the disease. The belief that cures for all diseases would be discovered due to our understanding of one's genes was also being disputed by scientists. Apparently, Doctor Steele was correct; environment was also a major factor.

As I walked across the newsroom, my thoughts wandered back to Sandra. I was thinking about the evening ahead when I remembered I still had a story to complete. A police officer had been shot earlier in the day, and I was supposed to visit the hospital to interview him. Hurrying out the door, I caught a cab and was soon on my way uptown.

When I reached the hospital, I made my way to the officer's room and found that it was a superficial wound and the officer would recover. Having completed the interview, I decided I would walk a block or two before hailing a cab and return to the paper. The Biocea building was located across the street, and I was curious to see what had become of it.

There was a biting winter chill in the air, causing me to bury my hands in my pockets, put my head down and hurry toward the front entrance. As I reached the building, it appeared as if everything was exactly the way it had been before Doctor Steele's death. I stood and stared at the building, watching the receptionist at the front desk rearranging some papers, knowing she would adamantly refuse to let me inside. Deciding to go around to the back of the building, I walked down the alleyway that led to the big black door. This was the same door Ngila had used to gain access to the city's streets all those months ago; the same door Sandra and I had used to escape.

I walked up to the door and pulled at the handle. It was locked, so I decided I would try knocking just to see if anybody would answer. After several raps, I surprisingly heard someone at the door fumbling with the lock. The door slowly opened with a screech, and a dark-haired woman with a sullen face cautiously stuck her head into the cold air.

I looked at the face, and immediately recognized her. "You're Doctor Steele's wife, aren't you?" I said.

The woman stared at me, apparently attempting to remember who I was. "Doctor Steele is dead," she finally replied. "And, yes, I was his wife. But who are you and why are you trying to enter through the back door?"

"You don't remember me? I'm Hudge Stone, the reporter who was there when your husband was killed in the fire."

Catherine looked at me with nervous apprehension. "Oh, yes, Mr. Stone, and what brings you back to Biocea?"

"I was just interested in the nature of the research being done here these days," I replied.

"I'm sorry, Mr. Stone, nothing that would interest you or your paper."

She uttered the words with a disturbing abruptness, accompanied by a disapproving frown. I realized she was about to push the door closed when I heard a gentle female voice calling my name from inside. I quickly planted my foot against the door, causing Catherine to sneer.

"Molly?" I called back.

"Yes, I'm in here!" she shouted.

I pushed the door open, and stepped past Catherine. "Are you all right? We've been searching for you for months."

A sudden look of despair crept across Molly's face. "The experiments," she said, "they've been completed."

"What do you mean?" I asked.

She turned and pointed at the large black door. "Let me show you," she said.

As I stepped forward, I heard a shrill scream from behind. "No, don't go in there!" shouted Catherine. Before I could answer, she had leaped upon my back, her hands flailing upon my head and shoulders.

Quickly stepping backward against the wall, I threw her from my back and she fell to the floor. Then I reached down and grabbed her arms, finally covering her mouth with one of my hands.

"In here," Molly anxiously whispered, opening the large black door.

Still holding Catherine, I slowly stepped into the room. There on the sofa was what appeared to be a baby wrapped in a white blanket.

"It's impossible," I murmured. "Is that?"

Molly nodded, a tear rolling down her cheek. "Yes, it's Ngila's child," she sobbed.

"But it can't be," I replied. "A child with a human mother?"

I let go of Catherine, and pushed her into the room. I then closed the door behind me.

"It's very possible," Catherine sneered. "My husband was a genius, can you understand that? Ngila was human, I tell you. The experiments were a success."

"Maybe," I replied. "But have you brought another murdering cannibal into the world?"

I watched as Molly walked toward me, the baby in her arms. She slowly pulled away the blanket exposing the infant's face. I noticed the high eyebrow-ridges, the broad nose, and large flat forehead.

"Looks exactly like Ngila," I whispered, as a sickening feeling spread through my stomach. The nightmare caused by the Project Dawning experiments was apparently not yet over.

"It's just so incredible," I said. "To think it was possible for a human to mate with Ngila. I wonder what Doctor Quant would say."

"He would realize the overwhelming significance," said Catherine. "Why, think of it, we now have the chance to study primitive man from the very beginning. We can watch him grow, begin to speak, why, study him through his entire life. I know this may seem wrong to you, but, believe me, I also initially resisted when Luther told me for the first time the truth about Project Dawning. But, in time, I came to see the importance of the experiments. You will, too."

"But it's unconscionable," I said. "There's no way I'm going to let another creature roam the streets of the city and kill innocent people. And what about all those other Ngilas you have cooking in those test tubes?"

"They will all be kept at Biocea," she replied. "No one will get hurt this time."

I looked at her, and reached for the cell phone I kept in my coat pocket.

"What are you doing?" demanded Catherine.

"Calling the police," I replied.

"But you can't," she snarled. "These experiments are invaluable to the progress of the human race."

"We'll see what the police have to say about that."

Catherine grimaced as I dialed the number. When the call was completed, she glared at me malevolently.

"Do you realize what you've just done?" she asked. "You've just destroyed years of hard work and planning that could have enormously benefited the human race."

"Better that than allowing you to experiment on another innocent creature, a creature, I might add, who just may be a natural born killer."

I looked down at the infant, and touched him with my finger. The baby gurgled for a moment, then unsheathed his tiny teeth and bit down on my finger. Recoiling in pain, I quickly withdrew my hand and examined it. Two tiny drops of blood oozed to the surface, and trickled down to my palm.

"So you still think he's harmless?" I asked.

I looked down at the baby, the pain still pulsing through my finger. A tiny rivulet of blood spilled from its lips to its tiny chin below.